SEX AND LIES

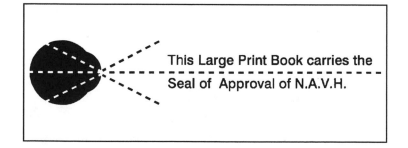

This Large Print Book carries the
Seal of Approval of N.A.V.H.

SEX AND LIES

DONNA HILL

THORNDIKE PRESS

A part of Gale, Cengage Learning

GALE
CENGAGE Learning™

Detroit • New York • San Francisco • New Haven, Conn • Waterville, Maine • London

GALE
CENGAGE Learning™

Copyright © 2008 by Donna Hill.
TLC (The Ladies Cartel Series #1).
Thorndike Press, a part of Gale, Cengage Learning.

Thorndike Press® Large Print African-American.
The text of this Large Print edition is unabridged.
Other aspects of the book may vary from the original edition.
Set in 16 pt. Plantin.
Printed on permanent paper.

LIBRARY OF CONGRESS CATALOGING-IN-PUBLICATION DATA

Hill, Donna (Donna O.)
    Sex and lies / by Donna Hill.
      p. cm. — (The ladies cartel series : no. 1) (Thorndike Press large print African-American)
    ISBN-13: 978-1-4104-1490-8 (alk. paper)
    ISBN-10: 1-4104-1490-6 (alk. paper)
    1. African Americans—Fiction. 2. New York (N.Y.)—Fiction. 3. Large type books. I. Title.
PS3558.I3864S49 2008
813'.54—dc22
                                 2008054023

Published in 2009 by arrangement with Harlequin Books S.A.

Printed in the United States of America
1 2 3 4 5 6 7 13 12 11 10 09

Dear Reader,
Welcome to my latest series, TLC (The Ladies Cartel). I had a great time crafting the first book of the series — *Sex and Lies.* This title reveals the torrid love and secrets between Savannah and her sexy husband, Blake. As the series continues, you'll get to know all the ladies who have a secret life and use their instincts as quickly as they use a gun or a listening device.

I have plenty of surprises in store, so be sure to collect the entire series. And guess what? You'll also get a chance to catch up with the ladies from PAUSE FOR MEN, who will drop by from time to time.

I hope you love The Ladies Cartel as much as you loved PAUSE FOR MEN. If you love sexy men, dynamic women, a hot plot and steamy sensuality, then you've come to the right place.

I'd love to hear what you think so far.

Please send me an e-mail at writerdoh@ aol.com with your thoughts!

Until the next installment, happy reading.

Donna Hill

To all my readers who have been so
supportive
over the years. I thank each and every
one of you
from the bottom of my heart.
                              Donna Hill

CHAPTER 1

Tonight would change her life. She knew it. Anticipation tingled in Savannah's veins. Had anyone asked her years earlier if she would ever be able to lead a double life, lie to family, friends and her husband about what she did in her spare time, she would have laughed in their faces. She spun her office chair away from her computer screen toward the ringing multiline phone.

"Billings and Tate, Attorneys-at-Law, Savannah Fields speaking."

"Hi, sweetheart," came the always chirpy voice.

"Hey, Mom." Savannah noticed the flashing blip on her computer screen from the corner of her eye, indicating a new e-mail. "What's up?" she asked as she opened the e-mail and read the note from her boss, Richard Billings. He needed a case file pulled to prepare for court. Savannah switched the call to her headset and walked to the file cabinet.

"I just wanted to remind you about the meeting tonight."

"I'll be there. I told Blake we were having our monthly pep meeting."

Mother and daughter chuckled.

"If Blake only knew what *TLC* really was," Claudia said.

"He'd have a fit." Savannah imagined the expression of appalled disbelief on her husband's face.

To the casual observer Savannah Fields was a highly paid paralegal for a small but busy corporate law firm in midtown Manhattan and married to Blake Fields, the very sexy architect and builder of upscale apartment complexes and office buildings. They lived a solid, upper-class lifestyle and enjoyed all of its perks. But Savannah, her mother and two dozen more New York women had a life that not even their closest friends would ever suspect.

"Well, tonight is important so try to get there early. I don't want you to miss out on anything and I want a good seat."

Savannah flipped through the files until she located the one she was looking for, then pushed the metal drawer shut. "You want me to pick you up?"

"No, I'll take my car."

"See you later, Mom, and no speeding," she warned. Claudia Martin was notorious for her lead foot.

Claudia scoffed at the reprimand. "I'll try."

"If you get there before I do, save me a seat. Gotta go. Love you." She smacked kisses into the phone before disconnecting the call.

"Savannah . . ."

She looked up into the deep-set green eyes of her boss, who was a dead ringer for an older version of the actor Keanu Reeves.

"Hey, Richard. I have that file for you." She reached for it on her desk and handed it over.

"Thanks. Look, I know this is short notice but I'm going to need you to stay a little longer tonight."

Her stomach knotted. "Tonight!" Her normally even timbre rose two octaves as she jerked her neck to the side.

Richard held up his hands and inadvertently took a step back. His friend and business partner Jack Tate had just been talking about a book by playwright and actor Tyler Perry — *Don't Make a Black Woman Take Off Her Earrings.* He might not be up on all the black vernacular, but he got the sense that if Savannah took off her earrings at this

11

precise moment he was in trouble.

"You know you will be paid well for the time. But I really need your help preparing for Monday."

Savannah pursed her lips and folded her arms beneath her C-cup breasts.

"Richard," she said, assuming her mother tone, "how many times have we been through this?" She pinched her lips and titled her head to the side.

Richard's hopeful expression turned sheepish. "I —"

She threw up her hand, palm facing Richard. "Don't answer. It was a rhetorical question. You can't keep waiting until the last minute. I know you're a brilliant attorney, which I hope to aspire to one day. But in the meantime I have a life, which begins promptly at 5:01 p.m." Her right brow rose to emphasize her point.

Richard took the well-deserved tongue lashing. They'd had this conversation at least once every couple of months for the past five years that they'd worked together. Savannah would chew him out, he took it and eventually she would help him out.

Any other time her "Richard traumas," which she'd dubbed these episodes, wouldn't be more than a minor annoyance, but today was different. However, she also knew that no matter what, Richard never asked her to do anything if he didn't really need her help — which was a lot.

Savannah blew out a breath. It was going to be a long night, but she could swing it.

"Fine," she conceded as they both knew she would. "But I'm warning you, I'm leaving at 7:00 p.m. sharp. And if you're not done then you explain to your client why he's going to jail."

Richard grinned, the dimple in his left cheek flashing. "Fair enough." He leaned down and kissed her forehead. "You're the best."

"I know," she grumbled, and reached for the ringing phone while waving Richard away.

"Billings and Tate . . ."

"Hey, baby."

Savannah's insides did a slow sensuous dance. Her eyes darkened and a warm smile moved languidly across her mouth.

"Hey, baby, yourself." She cuddled the phone close to her. "How's everything?"

"Busy as usual," Blake said with a light chuckle.

Savannah and Blake had been married for six years. Most people thought they were still newlyweds. Savannah adored her husband. He was the man she'd dreamed

13

about since she was a little girl and when they met at an out of the way lounge in the West Village she knew that dreams did come true.

The attraction between them from the very first night was comparable to what authors who write romance novels call "hot and instantaneous." Blake wasn't just good-looking — Blake Fields was *f-i-n-e,* with a capital *F.* It always amazed her that she was the one who landed him. She knew she was no showstopper. Actually she was quite ordinary looking and had to watch her weight with the diligence of a priest trying to save souls — it was an unending job. But she cleaned up well, as she would tell herself when she looked in the mirror. She knew all the makeup tricks and what clothes complemented her solid frame. More often than not, many people mistook her for Nia Long. Not to mention that Savannah could make Blake Fields see heaven when they made love.

"Busy is good," she said in response to his statement.

"I think I'm going to have some exciting news to share but I don't want to be premature."

Savannah grew jumpy with excitement. "You know I hate secrets," she pleaded, although she kept plenty herself. "Can't you at least give me a hint?"

"Okay, you beat it out of me." He cleared his throat. "Remember I told you about the housing-complex deal that was on the table?"

"Yes." Her pulse kicked up a notch and she held her breath. The housing complex would revitalize downtown Brooklyn and was touted to be the biggest single development in decades in the area.

"W-ell . . ." He drew out the word.

"Come on Blake," Savannah begged.

"We won the bid and they love my design."

"Blake!" she squealed, and jumped up from her seat. "Oh, my goodness, that's incredible. I knew you could do it, baby."

Blake laughed deep in his throat. "I am sailing! This is major. This project is so high profile. I'm going to be on the map for good."

"I'm so proud of you," she said, breaking down each word.

"This calls for a celebration. I thought we could go out tonight."

The wheels of elation came to a grinding halt.

"Tonight?" she croaked.

"Yeah." He paused. "Oh, you have that thing tonight."

She heard the disappointment in his voice. She squeezed her eyes shut and tried to think. There was no getting around missing the meeting at TLC, not to mention the extra time she would have to spend at work.

"Look, I'll be finished by nine, nine-thirty. It's Friday. Let's go for a late dinner and spend the day in bed tomorrow."

"Hmm, I like the sound of that already," he said, perking right up. "I'll make reservations at The Cabaret and I'll leave tomorrow in your very capable hands."

"Perfect," she purred into the phone. "I'll meet you at the restaurant no later than ten."

"Can't wait. I've been aching for you all day," Blake said, his voice growing thick.

Savannah squirmed in her seat and licked her lips. "I'll make it worth your while," she cooed.

"I intend to hold you to that. See you tonight."

"Love you," she whispered.

"Love you right back."

Slowly Savannah hung up the phone. Well, she certainly had her day cut out for her.

CHAPTER 2

Blake hung up the phone just as his assistant Jasmine poked her head in the partially open door.

"Blake, they're waiting for you in the conference room."

"Thanks, J. I'll be right there." He took his jacket from the back of his chair and put it on as he walked out. Jasmine handed him a manila folder as he passed her desk.

This meeting would be brief, Blake mused as he continued down the short hallway. Tristan Montgomery said she wanted to confirm some dates. That was something that could have easily been taken care of on the phone, but Ms. Montgomery never missed an opportunity to visit his office under one pretext or another.

"Sorry for the wait," he said, opening the door and stepping right inside. He shook hands with Tristan and then her latest assistant. As usual Tristan was dressed to exploit all of her attributes. Today it was a burnt orange number that dipped a little too low for nine to five.

"Not a problem," Tristan said. "Jasmine made us very comfortable." She let her eyes wander up and down his body.

Blake cleared his throat and smoothed down his tie as he sat. "So what do you need clarified, Ms. Montgomery?"

She pouted. "Please, Blake, we're in bed together, so to speak. You can at least call me Tristan." She rocked him with her expensive smile.

Blake sidestepped the comment and straightened his tie again. He opened the folder that Jasmine had given him before glancing up and across the hardwood table. Tristan was staring at him as if he were a rare delicacy that had been set on the table for lunch. He wanted to tug his tie off. It was suddenly cutting off his circulation. Being in the same room with Tristan Montgomery always did that to him.

She was one of the few black elite that was born into money. Her late father, Graham Montgomery built his fortune in the real-estate game. He'd started off by renting apartments for a small agency. Learning everything he could about investment property, he bought his first building at the age of twenty-five. Upon his untimely death at sixty-two, Graham Montgomery was a billionaire with property dotting across the country, from high-rise office buildings to luxury condos and strip malls. Before his death he started to stake a claim on one of the Hawaiian Islands. With his passing, his only child inherited it all.

"Uh, based on the rollout schedule I don't anticipate any problems," Blake said, keeping the conversation on track and his eyes on the documents in front of him.

Tristan slowly rose from her seat and rounded the table like a panther on the prowl until she stood slightly behind him. She placed her hand on his shoulder and leaned down to read the notes in front of him. Her left breast brushed his shoulder.

Blake tugged at his tie. "I was pretty sure that Jasmine gave you a copy," he said, trying to keep his voice light.

"You know how it is with copies . . ."

He was forced to look up at her. "No, actually I don't."

Tristan grinned and eased back. "They're nothing like the real thing," she said as she returned to her seat with the folder in her hand. She made show of reviewing the timeline.

"Were there any questions that you had in

particular?"

"Actually, yes." She flipped the folder shut. "With you being so busy with the design and overseeing construction, when will you ever have any free time?"

"Excuse me?" He couldn't believe that she went there — and in front of someone else. Maybe this was all some kind of game, a test of some sort.

"You know the old saying — all work and no play . . ."

"I'm sure I'll find time to relax. My main priority at the moment is getting this job up and running. That's it," he added, looking her deep in the eyes.

She lifted her chin ever so slightly. "I'm sure you have everything under control. But since it's my money that is financing it, I want to make sure that every *i* is dotted and every *t* is crossed."

"Of course. I can assure you that there is nothing to worry about." He glanced from one woman to the other then stood, hoping she would get the hint. "Is there anything else that we need to discuss?"

"Yes, your availability next week."

He frowned. "Excuse me?"

"I'm hosting a dinner party at my penthouse next week." She picked up her clutch purse from the table. "There are several people I want you to meet, potential clients."

"Sounds wonderful. Both me and my wife, Savannah, love dinner parties." He reached across the table, snatched up the folder and tucked it beneath his arm.

Her eyes tightened just a hint. "I'll be sure to get all the details to Jasmine."

"Great. I'll walk you both to the elevator." He held the door open for her. When she passed she ran her hand along the sleeve of his suit jacket.

"Armani?"

Blake swallowed. "Yes."

She grinned, her hazel eyes darkened. "I can always tell. You're a man with good taste. I like that in a man." She brushed by him and walked out.

Once they were gone, Blake released his long breath of tension. He stopped at Jasmine's desk. "Listen, the next time that woman comes here you make sure you buzz me after five minutes."

Jasmine tried not to laugh. "Don't tell me she hit on you."

"I won't." He walked off to his office.

Once inside the safety of his own space, he took his tie off completely. Tristan was a gorgeous woman there was no doubt about that. And he knew a come on when he saw one. In all the years of his marriage he had never strayed or contemplated straying. He was more than happy with Savannah and he didn't need the distraction of a hot socialite to ruin his track record. He certainly hoped that Ms. Montgomery stayed on her side of the dividing line. Mixing business with pleasure could bring nothing but trouble.

He reached for the phone to make reservations for dinner. A pleasant dinner with his wife and a long night of good loving was just the thing he needed to dislodge the memory of Tristan's lush body brushing up against his.

Just as he finished with his phone call and had his reservation confirmed for ten, his close friend and business partner, Steven Long, knocked on the door.

"Come in." He hung up the phone. "Hey, man."

"Hey, yourself." He stepped inside. "I got a whiff of Ms. Hotstuff." He chuckled. "What brings her to our neck of the woods again?"

"Nothing that couldn't have been handled on the phone. She claimed she wanted to go over the rollout schedule."

"But what she really wanted was to roll you out." He plopped down in a chair opposite Blake.

"Very funny."

"But true. That woman has a thing for you, man. Every time you step into the room her eyes light up."

Blake grimaced. "I'm a married man."

"I really don't think she cares."

"Is it that obvious that she's . . ."

"I'll put it this way, even Stevie Wonder could see it."

Blake shook his head. "I'm trying to keep this all on the up and up. The last thing I need is to get our wires crossed."

"Like I said, she doesn't care. But, hey, if you don't want it feel free to send her in my direction. I sure as hell wouldn't throw her out of bed."

Steve was a notorious hound from back in their college days at Moorehouse University. He'd slowed down just a little when they headed off to MIT for grad school where they received their engineering and architectural degrees, but Steven still needed a secretary to keep up with the women he dated. Not much had changed in the years since. It totally escaped Blake why Tristan had latched on to him and not Steven who was single and always available.

"She's having some kind of gathering at her penthouse next week."

"You know how I love hotsy-totsy parties," he joked.

"Yeah, anyway, she's supposed to send over the information to Jasmine. Said she has some people she wants me to meet — potential business."

Steven nodded. "Cool. I'll pencil her in. Wonder if she is going to have any of her rich, single girlfriends around."

Blake held up his hand. "Don't even think about it. I don't want to screw up this deal when some fling of yours goes bad — as they tend to do."

Steven held his hand to his chest. "You wound me, dawg. Can I help it if I have a short attention span and the ladies can't take goodbye for an answer?"

"Whatever. Just don't mess this up."

"I don't think it's me you have to worry about. Ms. Thing isn't one to take no for an answer and sooner or later she's gonna want yours."

Blake shot him a look of disregard but the truth of the matter was that Steven was right.

CHAPTER 3

Savannah's three-inch heels clicked like shotgun fire against the concrete of the underground employee parking lot. Her navy blue skirt suit with the pristine white tank top and a strand of real pearls around her slender neck gave her the appearance of the legal eagle she could easily become.

For a woman of only five foot five she had a long stride. She swore it came from her devout adherence to Pilates. She believed she could use all the help she could get in keeping her weight under control and giving her compact body more of a sleek and lean appearance. And as she had come to discover since becoming a member of TLC, looks were definitely deceiving.

She used her remote to disengage the alarm on her black SUV and hopped up inside. The garage had a few cars left of those still burning the after-hour oil. She checked the dashboard clock against her watch — seven-forty. She cussed under her breath and put the SUV in gear, her skirt rising up her thighs to a provocative level. She'd wound up staying longer than she'd planned and now she would really have to make double-time.

Quickly maneuvering around pillars and yellow directional arrows, she used her monthly pass card and zipped up the exit ramp and out into the approaching twilight. As she made her way to the FDR she silently prayed that traffic would be light. She entered the FDR from 34th Street and went north. Thankfully there was an open lane and she grinned as she watched the speedometer climb to 70 mph. At that pace she'd reach Harlem in about fifteen minutes.

In record time, she pulled onto the street that housed TLC headquarters, which was tucked away in an upscale brownstone directly across the street from the Pause for Men day spa. If she wasn't a married woman she could certainly spend her free time man watching with all the hotties that came in and out of there. Of course, parking was at a premium and it took her another five minutes to find a spot a block away.

Savannah checked in at reception, showing her ID, and then went upstairs to where the meeting was being held.

The main room was buzzing with chatter from the members of TLC who were using the time to catch up and share stories before the formal meeting began. Savannah waved to Leslie and Dina, two of the women she recognized. They were both high up in the ranking, having been part of TLC for about five years. As a result they got the best assignments. Savannah's goal was to one day be on par with both of them.

She walked over to the refreshment table and poured herself a cup of fruit punch just as Claudia came up behind her.

"I was wondering when you were going to get here."

Savannah turned to see her mother. As always Claudia Martin was ready for her close-up. Claudia, unlike Savannah was tall and still slender. Her skin was butter soft, the color of warm honey and so flawless the only makeup she ever used was lipstick and mascara. Both mother and daughter loved clothes by St. John and Claudia wore hers well. Tonight she chose a red jersey sheath with a matching jacket. Gold was her accessory.

Savannah leaned up and kissed her mother's cheek. "Richard had a last-minute project."

Claudia made a face. "What else is new? One of these days you need to tell him just where he can go."

"Mom!" Savannah scoffed and bit back a laugh. "He's my boss and it's my job."

Claudia waved off the comment. "Humph."

"Ladies, if everyone could take their seats we're ready to get started," Leslie announced from the small podium.

Claudia grabbed Savannah by the arm and hustled her to the front. "I got us a spot on the antique loveseat."

The main room or ballroom of the brownstone was set up like an English parlor, with heavily decorated seating in a variety of brocades and velvets, crystal chandeliers, mahogany tables, gilded mirrors and a marble fireplace. It was like stepping back in time.

Savannah and Claudia took their seats. After several moments of shuffling and jockeying, the rest of the women found seats and settled down. As Savannah surveyed the assemblage she was still intrigued by the array of women who made up TLC — everything from business executives to fashion models, housewives to single mothers and in all shapes, sizes and nationalities.

To everyone outside of the elite organization TLC meant Tender Loving Care body products and its members were the equivalent of Avon or Amway sales reps. They were far from it.

"The June meeting of The Ladies Cartel will now come to order," Leslie announced. "We have a great deal to cover tonight — old business and new assignments."

Claudia squeezed Savannah's hand with anticipation. Savannah felt the rush of adrenaline. If she was lucky she would get her first assignment. She'd only been with the organization for a little under a year but in that time she'd made great strides in learning the intricacies of the Cartel's operation; self-defense techniques, surveillance equipment and how to shoot a gun if necessary. She'd been recruited by her mother and she couldn't have been more stunned than if her mother announced that she was indeed Santa Claus.

It was a Saturday afternoon; mother and daughter were in the local supermarket shopping for their annual Fourth of July barbecue. As they were loading their packages into Savannah's SUV, Claudia out of the blue said that she was a member of a secret organization.

"What?" Savannah laughed. "What secret

organization, shoppers anonymous?" Claudia was a relentless shopper, her passion for clothes and home furnishings boggled Savannah's mind.

"I'm serious," she said. "And I have been allowed to recruit someone and I want that someone to be you."

"Ma, what in the world are you talking about?" Savannah put the last bag in the car and got in behind the wheel. She put on her designer sunglasses and pulled off.

"Just listen. Four years ago I met a woman in my exercise class, Dina Fleming. She told me about this group of women who are hired to perform a variety of jobs — mostly surveillance but sometimes it's more involved. It could be anything from posing as a girlfriend to getting hired at a business to find out about illegal practices."

Savannah turned to her mother in disbelief, peering at her over the top of her shades.

"I've done several jobs myself," she said with pride.

"Are you kidding me?"

"No. Remember the big scandal about the child-care agency about a year ago?"

Savannah frowned as she tried to remember. "Sort of, why?"

"I worked that case."

Savannah tossed her head back and laughed. "Stop playing."

"I'm very serious. There are about thirty women who are part of the Cartel — in the New York chapter. For those outside of the circle they believe we are no more than a group of women who sell skin-care and body products. No one ever suspects us, that's why we're so successful at what we do."

Maybe her mother was getting senile, Savannah thought as she drove and listened to the absurd story. She'd seen her mother's case of bath and beauty products hundreds of times. Now she expected her to think it was all part of some elite organization?

"Do you really expect me to believe this? Is this some gimmick to recruit me to sell something?"

"I promise you it's not. I presented your credentials to the board and they want to meet you."

"Credentials?"

"The fact that you work for a law firm and are familiar with the law, attorneys and the court system, we believe you could be a major asset to the organization."

Her head was spinning. This was nonsense, but she figured the least she could do was humor her mother. "Mom, I'm sure you really believe all this and if it will make you feel better I'll meet your friends." She patted her mother's thigh.

Claudia pushed her daughter's hand away. "Don't patronize me! I'm not some blithering idiot. And you should know better." She folded her arms in a huff. "If I'd thought for a minute that you would react this way I would have never opened my mouth."

Savannah stole a glance at her mother and could tell by the hard set of her mouth and the deep furrow between her brows that she was dead serious.

"I'm sorry if I offended you, Mom, but you have to admit this all sounds crazy."

"I know, I thought the same thing. But it's real, very real. So are you interested?"

"Intrigued, for sure."

"Good." Her expression brightened. "I'll set everything up."

And she did. Savannah met with Dina and Leslie and was grilled as if she were applying for a job with the CIA. Then they did a background check and when everything came back clear she began her training which lasted for six months.

TLC was a secret society of highly skilled women who were hired to perform covert operations at the behest of scorned wives, jealous husbands, business executives, government agencies and families in dispute over inheritances. It came into being more than a decade earlier, having started in Langley, Virginia — home to secrets and lies. What began as a small investigative firm headed by Jean Wallington, slowly mush-roomed into TLC with branches all across the country.

Savannah was ready for her very first assignment and she hoped that tonight would be the night.

"I want to begin by congratulating Tina and Marilyn for the excellent job they did with the redlining that was happening on Long Island," Leslie said. "As a result of their hard work, the real-estate agency that was discriminating against single women home owners and black families has been closed and the owners are facing jail time."

A cheer followed by applause filled the room.

"Brenda Levin has been promoted to level two for her hard work in recruiting the most new members in the past year."

More applause.

"Tonight I want you all to give a warm welcome to three new recruits. When I call your names will you please stand? Margaret Jacobs, Mi Lin Chan and Denise Walker."

The ladies stood, smiled and waved at

their fellow Cartel members to shouts of "Welcome aboard."

Leslie waited until the room quieted. She scanned the room. "As you know from the monthly newsletter that comes with your supplies, we have several cases that need our attention. The board has reviewed the experience, skills and personal backgrounds of each of you and we've made our selections." Leslie cleared her throat and tucked several strands of her blond hair behind her ear. She opened a leather folder and pulled out a piece of paper. The room hushed.

"Serena Hamilton, Justine Parker and Savannah Fields."

The collected held breath was released. Savannah clutched her mother's hand, animation sparkling in her eyes.

"Each of you ladies will receive your instructions before you leave tonight. Of course, after reading what is required of you, you have the option to decline the assignment. Should you decide to take the assignment you will be provided with whatever support the Cartel can provide. Congratulations, ladies, and with that this portion of the meeting is adjourned. Feel free to enjoy the food and drinks and would Serena, Justine and Savannah stop in the office before you leave." Leslie stepped away from the podium and chatter filled the room.

"Congratulations, Savannah," Melonie, one of the early members of the Cartel said. "This is your first assignment, right?"

"Yes, it is." Savannah was giddy with excitement. Her mind was running in a million directions at once trying to imagine what her assignment would be.

Melonie touched Savannah's shoulder. "Well, if you need anything let me know, but you have a pro in the family," she added, looking with admiration at Claudia. "So I'm sure you'll be fine."

Savannah drew in a long breath. "That I do."

They chatted for a few minutes more and Savannah continued to get words of encouragement and support from her sister members.

Claudia yawned. "Sorry," she said. "Long day."

Savannah looked at her watch and gasped in alarm. It was nine forty-five. She'd promised Blake she would meet him at the restaurant at ten and she still had to meet with Leslie to get her assignment.

"I really have to go. I have a dinner date with my husband."

"Go, girl, go," Melonie said.

"Let me check in with Leslie. Mom, I'll

call you tomorrow." She kissed her mother's cheek, said her goodbyes and hurried to the main office which was down the hallway from the ballroom.

When she got to the office, Justine was just coming out. "Good luck," she murmured as she passed Savannah.

"Thanks, you, too."

Savannah stepped up to the closed door and knocked lightly.

"Come in," came the voice on the other side of the door.

Savannah turned the knob and stepped inside. For an instant her step faltered. It wasn't Leslie as she'd expected but the head honcho in charge.

"Savannah." Jean Wallington beamed as if she'd run into a long-lost friend. "Come in. Have a seat."

Jean Wallington rarely made an appearance. She was so high up the chain of command that you needed oxygen to hang out with her. Word had it that she was a former CIA operative who'd specialized in covert ops. Having had her fill with the old boys' club she, over time, began recruiting for her own organization. Jean firmly believed that women had just as much, if not more, skill in the field of undercover operations, primarily because no one ever suspected a woman. But mostly because women understood people. Women had instincts and they were rarely wrong. Jean banked on those instincts of her team to get the jobs done. She was never wrong.

Savannah flashed a nervous smile and sat in the high back Queen Ann chair opposite Jean. Jean folded her hands on top of the cherrywood desk.

"I've been watching you for a while, Savannah," Jean began, "and I'm very impressed by what I've seen."

"Thank you."

Jean flipped open a thin manila file folder and quickly glanced over it before sweeping her thin pink-framed glasses from her sharp nose, displaying the most intense green eyes Savannah had ever seen. They were the color of jade.

"When we make our selections, we do it very carefully. We take many factors into account — length of membership, who you were recruited by, your education, profession and how you did during training. Most important we look at what we call the unobvious skills or attributes in our members." Jean waved her glasses toward Savannah. "In your case we discovered that you have an innate quality with people. People are drawn to you, Savannah, and for this assignment that's exactly what we need — that, combined with your legal background. We feel you are the perfect member to handle this job."

Savannah had no idea that she was viewed that way. She was thrilled to know it yet a bit unsettled to realize that she'd been watched that closely without her knowledge. Damn, they were good.

"Your assignment will be to gather evidence on The Montgomery Enterprises. It has been brought to our attention that the corporation has been laundering money in addition to working with substandard products in the development of their housing projects and some corporate structures. We're confident that the confirmation we're seeking is buried in their legal documents. They have some of the best lawyers in the country on their payroll." She took a larger manila envelope from the file and handed it over to Savannah. "All of the information you need is inside. The information on those pages will begin to dissolve within fifteen minutes of opening the envelope and exposing it to the air. Memorize it. The tools that you need will be delivered to you in your next TLC shipment by courier."

Savannah nodded. The name Montgomery gave her an itch that she couldn't quite scratch. It was so familiar but she wasn't sure why. She held the envelope to her chest. Her racing heart thumped making the envelope vibrate like a tuning fork.

"Any questions?"

"How much time do I have?"

"Three weeks."

Savannah's deep brown eyes widened a fraction.

"Of course, you will have the full support of TLC."

"Any reason for the short window?"

"Yes, The Montgomery Enterprises is set to break ground on a new development by the end of the month. We need the information irrefutably verified before then."

Montgomery . . . breaking ground. It couldn't be.

"If there's nothing else." Jean stood and Savannah realized for the first time just how tall Jean actually was. She had to be at least five-eleven, Savannah guesstimated. She got up, took the envelope still clutched to her chest and stuck out her hand. "Thank you for the opportunity, Jean."

"I expect great things from all of our Cartel members," she said, shaking Savannah's hand with a death grip, her green eyes boring into Savannah's.

"I won't disappoint you."

"I know."

Savannah drew in a short breath and lifted her chin an inch in acceptance.

With her first assignment plastered to the front of her suit jacket by a damp hand, Savannah bobbed and weaved her way out of the brownstone, accepting heartfelt congratulations along the way. Once outside she gulped in the night air then sprinted down the street to her car. It was already ten-twenty. She got in the car and immediately called Blake on her cell phone.

"Baby, I'm so sorry," she said the instant his voice came on the phone.

"No worries, sugar. I ran into Mac and we were having a drink at the bar. How much longer will you be?"

"At least fifteen minutes."

"See you when you get here."

"Love you," Savannah said, truly meaning it.

"Back at ya. Drive safe."

She flipped the phone closed and put the car in gear. Her husband was the best. Damn she was lucky.

At least up to that point.

CHAPTER 4

The Cabaret restaurant and lounge was located on the upper Eastside of Manhattan on Park Avenue and 52nd Street. Blake and Savannah had stumbled upon this jewel during the first year of their marriage when they were still exploring each other and the city that they loved. The Cabaret became "their place" and they celebrated every event worth celebrating there.

The food was exquisite, though pricey, but it was the atmosphere that drew them back time and again. It had just the right amount of dim lighting with mirrors in strategic places, candle votives on the intimate tables tucked throughout the space. And every night there was a great jazz performance.

"So how's married life, my man?" Mac asked as he swallowed what remained of his vodka on the rocks.

Blake grinned. "Couldn't be better. I love it."

"Get out. You, Mr. Permanent Bachelor." Mac chuckled.

Blake lowered his head, his grin broadening. "Yeah, I didn't figure marriage was for me, but when I met Savannah . . ." He shook his head in wonder. "All the others paled in comparison to her."

"I can't believe it. I have women still asking me about 'your friend, um, Blake,' " he said in a really bad falsetto.

They laughed at Mac's bad imitation of a female voice.

"I'm off the market, man." Blake took a swig of his drink. "What about you, ever going to settle down?"

"Why?" He signaled the waiter for another drink. "I firmly believe that men were not created to be with one woman. Why do you think they outnumber us?"

Blake cut his eyes in Mac's direction and snorted a laugh. "Maybe because we drop dead sooner from trying to keep up with so many women."

"But what a way to go!"

They clinked glasses.

"Other than women how're things going on The Street?"

Mac, whose real name was Fred McDonald, worked on Wall Street. They were both Moorehouse grads, but Blake had gone

42

on to study architecture at MIT. After graduation, Mac went to work buying and selling.

"Crazy man. The work is grueling but the rewards are worth it. Just bought my second house out in Montclair, New Jersey."

"Congratulations! But what are you going to do with two homes?"

"The brownstone in Harlem is strictly an investment property. The one in Jersey is where I'll live."

"You plan to commute into New York every day? The traffic is horrific."

"Naw, I have enough stress to deal with at work. I'll be using mass transit."

Blake nodded. "Good move."

"What's going on with you?"

"Just landed a major development deal."

"Yeah, which one?" He angled his body on the stool toward Blake.

"Can't really talk about it right now. The ink is still drying. But I will say that it will put me on the map for good."

Mac slapped him on the back. "I always knew you would hit the big-time."

"That's what Savannah and I are celebrating tonight." He brought his glass to his mouth and took a slow swallow.

"It'll be good to see Savannah again. We all have to get together sometime. You and

Savannah and me and whomever I'm so inclined to be with at the moment." He chuckled.

Blake shook his head. "One of these days the right woman is gonna come along and you will be toast."

"Like you were toast . . ." Savannah whispered in Blake's ear. She pecked him on the cheek. "Sorry I'm late."

Blake swiveled around on the stool and wrapped his arms around her waist. "Hey, baby." His gaze danced over her face still amazed that this woman was all his. He tenderly kissed her mouth.

"Hey, get a room," Mac jokingly cut in.

"Don't hate," Savannah teased, stepping out of her husband's arms. She came around her husband and hugged Mac. "Good to see you." She patted his arm. "Still on the prowl?" she asked, referring to his notorious womanizing.

"Like the old saying goes, can't teach an old dog new tricks."

Blake slid off the stool and turned to Mac. "Let's get together soon. It's been a long time."

Mac stuck out his hand which Blake shook. "Definitely. Give me a call anytime. All of my numbers are the same."

"I will," Blake said.

"Good seeing you, Savannah," Mac said.

"You, too," Savannah replied.

Blake slid his arm around her waist. "Our table is waiting. Let me tell the hostess you're here."

They walked to the front of the restaurant. The hostess approached.

"My party has arrived," Blake said.

"Great. Right this way." She took two menus from the holder and led them to their table. "Your server will be with you shortly. Can I get you something to drink in the meantime?"

Blake held up his glass. "I'm good." He turned to Savannah.

"Hmm, I'll have a diet cola with a twist of lemon."

"Your server will be right here with your drink and to take your orders. Have a good evening."

Blake turned his full attention to his wife. "You have that gleam in your eyes. Something exciting happen at work or at your meeting?"

Savannah inwardly flinched. "Nothing out of the ordinary. I'm buzzed about you!" She reached across the table and squeezed his hand. "Tell me everything — or at least as much as you can," she said.

"Well, all systems are go on the development. The entire project has been kept under wraps for months, as you know. There's been so much speculation about who was going to get the contract, if all the money would come through in time and if the City Council would approve it." He blew out a breath. "It's been an uphill battle the entire time. The surrounding community has been against it from the beginning." The light in his eyes slowly dimmed. He looked at his wife. "Some folks are going to lose their homes."

Savannah heard the sadness in his voice. "But when the project is done, it will be better than before," she said, hoping to lift some of the weight off his shoulders. "And this project is going to provide jobs for thousands, especially minorities."

The corner of his lush mouth curved up in a grin. "You sound like the Mayor's press secretary."

She waved off his comment with a light chuckle. "I don't mean to sound like the poster child for redevelopment, but it will ultimately improve the area, bring in jobs and housing. Isn't the city planning to provide relocation support to anyone who becomes displaced?"

"That's what we've been told."

"Then stop worrying. Enjoy your fifteen

minutes of fame and put up the best damned development that this town has seen in decades."

"That's why I love you."

She lowered her lids and looked at him coyly. "And why is that?"

" 'Cause you always know how to make me feel good in and out of bed," he said.

Her voice dropped to a husky whisper. "We all have our skills." She puckered her lips and blew him a kiss.

"Are you ready to order?"

Two pairs of eyes rose to meet those of the waitress.

"We're not hungry," they said in unison.

Blake sliced a look at his wife. "You can bring the check for the drinks."

Blake and Savannah tumbled through the door of their Harlem town house, giggling and groping like teenagers. The entire drive home Blake had kept one hand on the wheel and the other buried between his wife's thighs. If there weren't so many bright street lights on their block they would have made love right there in the front seat of the car. But being the respectable couple that they thought themselves to be, it wouldn't look good to get caught by one of the members of the block patrol.

Savannah kicked the door shut and tugged at Blake's shirt. Two white buttons went dancing across the sparkling hardwood floor. His tie dangled at an angle from around his neck. Blake grabbed the hem of her skirt and hitched it up around her hips. Mouths and tongues sought out any inch of exposed flesh as they tore off clothes en route to the bedroom.

Savannah and Blake tumbled onto the king-size bed, she pinned snuggly beneath his hard body.

"This is all I could think about all day," he murmured in her ear before nibbling her lobe.

"Show me exactly what you were thinking about," she whispered back.

The sublime pleasure that Blake evoked in her body hadn't waned a bit in the years of their marriage. If anything her lust and passion for him seemed to have escalated with time. He knew every one of her buttons and he expertly pressed them all until she was feverish with need.

His fingertips were featherlight as they glided and caressed her hot flesh. His mouth teased and taunted the slope of her neck, inching downward to the rise of her breasts before taking a tight nipple into his mouth and laving it with his tongue.

Savannah moaned, a sound that was filled with urgency, but Blake took his time — the scenic route as he called it — and continued to chart new territory. He slipped his hand between her parted thighs and flicked his finger back and forth across her swollen bud until her entire body trembled.

Blake reluctantly left the tenderness of her breasts and eased down toward her fluttering stomach, letting his tongue dance around her navel.

Savannah's hips instinctively moved in a slow undulating fashion. *Please* escaped from her lips on a rush of hot breath.

"This what you want?" he uttered just as his tongue slid across the pulse of her bud.

Savannah cried out and gripped the sheets in tight fists. Her pelvis jutted upward and Blake grabbed her behind and pulled her fully toward his eager mouth. He suckled and teased until he knew from her tortured mewls and the shuddering of her body that she was ready to explode into a million tiny pieces. He pushed her thighs farther apart then up and over his shoulders.

Hot tears squeezed out of her eyes as she was suddenly filled with the rock hardness of her husband. He moved into her by degrees giving them both a chance to savor those first moments of unity.

"Oh," he groaned deep in his throat. "You're so hot . . . so wet." He pushed in farther and she squeezed around him while rotating her hips.

Savannah reached down between them and found his heavy, seed-filled sac and gently massaged it. Blake plunged deep inside her until there was nowhere else to go but in and out on a maddening quest to reach heaven.

Their paced picked up in unison. Savannah swore she heard ringing in her ears, every nerve ending in her body was charged. Her head swam. And then Blake did that thing he always did. He moved inside her in a circle and hit that spot.

Lights erupted. Her entire body stiffened for several seconds as if electrified. Then her *insides,* with a mind of their own, violently contracted and released around his stiff member. It felt as if he were growing inside her as he approached his own climax which set off another wave of contractions that spread up her belly and out to her limbs to explode in her brain.

She opened her mouth to scream out her pleasure, but all sound was trapped in her throat as her climax spun out of control. Blake rode her faster and faster, the words coming from his lips incomprehensible. He pulled her so close to his wet body that not even air separated them as he pushed and pushed and pushed. He buried his head into the valley of her neck barely muffling the growl of release that jettisoned from him into her.

Maybe this time, Savannah silently prayed as she clung to her husband, concentration on draining him of every ounce of his fertile seed, keeping her hips high in the air. *Maybe this time.* She felt him pulse and jerk inside her. She wrapped her legs tightly around him and used her hand to press him against her opening, not allowing even a drop to escape.

"I love you so much," Blake whispered, his voice cracking with emotion. His body convulsed one last time before all his weight eased down on her, pinning her to the damp sheets.

"And I love you, my darling man. I love you."

They closed their eyes, holding on to each other, locked as one.

CHAPTER 5

"We didn't get a chance to talk much last night," Blake said with a wicked grin on his face as he emerged from the shower with a towel wrapped around his waist.

Savannah had her knees drawn up to her chest, watching her handsome husband approach and wondered how she'd gotten so lucky. She angled her head to the side. "I think we did a lot of talking, just not the verbal kind."

He pointed a finger in her direction. "Touché."

Savannah patted an empty spot next to her. "So tell me about the deal."

Blake came to sit beside her. He fluffed up a pillow and leaned back against it, folding his hands across his sculpted belly.

"Well, as I was hinting at . . ."

He explained the details of the deal which entailed his company being the sole architect for the project, as well as handling the contract for finding the right construction crew.

"How long will the entire project last from start to finish?"

"If we get all the clearances on time and I can seal a deal with the contractors . . . Hmm, from start to finish, at least a year. And that's barring all of the unforeseen obstacles that come up with any job this size."

Savannah nodded. "Did I tell you how proud I am of you?"

Blake snuggled close. "Probably so, but tell me again."

She cupped his chin in her palm. "I'm so proud of you." She pecked him on the lips then winked.

"And how did your meeting go with the ladies last night?" He yawned loudly and threw his arm across his eyes. "What I wouldn't give to be a fly on the wall."

Savannah's heart thumped then settled. She still had not read the details of her assignment. But she had a very strong feeling that it wasn't going to be easy. "It went fine as usual. Girl stuff. Uh, honey . . ."

"Hmm?"

"What is the name of the finance people for the development again? Did you say Montgomery?"

"Yeah, The Montgomery Enterprises. Run by Miss Conglomerate herself, Tristan Montgomery."

Lord, please don't let it be her.

"By the way, she invited us to a get together at her home next week."

"Really? Then she can't be all that bad."

"I don't know what it is about the woman that rubs me the wrong way."

"But you don't work with her directly. So it shouldn't be too much of a problem."

"That's just it — I don't. But she's what you call a 'hands on' person. She's up on every detail, no matter how small."

"Don't let it bother you. She probably thinks she has to try harder because she's a woman."

"Hmm, maybe. Anyway, I don't want to talk business today. It's our day off. So what do you want to do today?"

"I was reading in the *Village Voice* that there's a boat ride up the Hudson from nine to one. Wanna go?"

"Sounds great." He turned on his side to face her. "That leaves us with quite a few hours to kill. Got any ideas on what we could do?" he asked as he trailed a finger down the center of her chest.

"We could try again to make a miracle happen." Her eyes looked at him from the depths of her soul.

Blake stroked her cheek. He knew how desperately Savannah wanted a child. They'd been trying unsuccessfully for nearly a year. He saw the sadness in her eyes when every month she'd stay as regular as a Swiss clock. They could buy stock in those little testing sticks with the amount of money she'd spent on in-home pregnancy tests.

"Listen, I don't want you to make yourself crazy about getting pregnant. The doctor said it could take time."

She pushed out a sigh. "I know." Her tone was full of dejection. "It's just that every time we make love I keep hoping . . . ya know?"

He kissed her tenderly. "I know. And when the time is right, it will happen." He rolled gently on top of her. "But in the meantime you know the old saying of practice makes perfect." He stroked her hip.

Savannah giggled. "Yeah, I had heard something like that . . ."

And as she took her husband deep into her body once more, she sent up her continued chant, *maybe this time.*

Savannah was in the kitchen fixing them something to eat before they both passed out from hunger and sexual fatigue when the phone rang.

"I got it," Blake yelled out from the bedroom where he hadn't moved from since they woke up.

Several moments later she could hear him coming up behind her chuckling and saying, "yes, ma'am." He handed her the phone. "Mom." He turned and sauntered back to the bedroom.

"Hey, Mom." She tucked the phone between her ear and shoulder and continued to fix the western omelet.

"Hey, sweetie, can you talk?"

Savannah took a quick glance over her shoulder. "Yep. What's up?"

"You tell me," her mother said in a conspiratorial whisper.

Savannah lowered her voice. "I didn't get a chance to look at it yet."

"What? Savannah," she said in that tone she used with her as a little girl. "This is important. You wouldn't have been chosen if they didn't completely believe in you."

"Mother, I know. It's just that . . . well, I've been a little tied up."

Her mother said, "Chile, you're going to kill that man one of these days."

Savannah bit back a laugh. It never ceased to amaze her how out there and open her mother was about sex. "We are trying to have a baby, so I never want to miss out on an opportunity."

She turned off the flame beneath the frying pan and placed the omelet onto a platter. Savory steam wafted up to her nose.

"I told you before, stop trying and it will happen."

Savannah sighed. "Yeah, that's what Blake keeps saying."

"And he's right. Relax, sweetheart. I know you and Blake will make beautiful babies together when the time is right. In the meantime, I suggest you take a look at your assignment. I want you to do well on this. People are depending on you."

Savannah swallowed hard. "I'll take care of it. Promise."

"Good, and if you need me for anything, let me know."

"I will."

"Love you."

"Love you, too."

Slowly Savannah hung up the phone then took the platter and put it on the kitchen table. A part of her desperately wanted to read what was inside that envelope and another part of her dreaded it. But if she only had three weeks to pull off whatever it was that needed to be done, she couldn't ignore the contents for long.

CHAPTER 6

"I'm just going to relax and watch the game," Blake said, assuming his Sunday-afternoon position on the couch.

What else is new, Savannah's arched brow queried. She walked by and handed him the remote. It was a ritual she'd grown used to since the beginning of their marriage. Blake was willing to give all of his time and energy to her Monday through Saturday, but Sunday was sports day come hell or high water.

"Can I get you anything?" she asked.

"No, I'm good." He'd already spread out his goodies for the afternoon — chips, pretzels and an ice bucket with beer — and was surfing through the stations. The blare of a baseball game filled the room.

Savannah leaned down and kissed his forehead then headed off to the bedroom. She closed the door behind her. Going to her dresser, she opened the bottom drawer and pulled out the envelope that was tucked beneath her lingerie.

Taking it to the bed, she felt her heart pound with trepidation. She used a nail file to slit open the top then pulled out the stapled pages. It had the TLC logo blazoned across the top. She knew she only had a short period of time to digest all of the information that was contained in the hermetically sealed envelope before the letters on the pages began to dissolve.

She read quickly, absorbing the information the way she did legal briefs, cataloging everything that was important and discarding the rest.

The more she read, the more disturbed she became. What she'd feared was no longer a bad feeling. It was a full-blown reality. The knot that had settled in her stomach since she'd gotten her assignment from Jean now threatened to loop around her lungs and cut off her air.

Her assignment was to infiltrate Montgomery headquarters on East 72nd Street, secure the original accounting documents and the legal papers that negotiated the land-acquisition deal for the development in downtown Brooklyn — the project that her husband was working on. It was believed that not only was The Montgomery Enterprises involved in illegal land deals and coercion, but several members of the City Council and the architect and developer, i.e. Blake Fields, PPC. She was to secure the necessary documents, any video tapes or audio conversations that would lead to indictments of all the parties involved — or irrefutable information to exclude them.

Her stomach roiled. Bile rose to the back of her throat and sat there burning. She stared at the pages as the words began to cloud over. She wiped the tears from her eyes as she watched the words slowly become ghostlike on the page until they were totally gone. The only thing remaining was the TLC logo.

The sudden ringing of the phone snapped through her, jerking her out of the place to which she'd descended. Dully she turned toward the intruding instrument and picked it up. She cleared her throat and sniffed hard.

"Hello . . ."

"Damn, girl, it's nearly one in the afternoon, you still sleep?"

Savannah laughed. Danielle Holloway was one of her two best friends, notorious for her early morning wake-up calls. One o'clock was definitely late for Dani. "What's up? And no, I'm not still asleep. Are you ill? It's after ten." She stole a glance at the now lily white pages.

"Very funny. I figured I'd give you a play since it was Sunday and all. Got any plans for today?"

"Not really. You know today is Blake's sports day, so I'm pretty much off of his radar until bedtime."

"I just got off the phone with Nia, we were thinking about going down to the South Street Seaport. They're having a jazz concert on one of the boats."

Maybe getting out of the house for the day and spending it with her girls was just the thing she needed to clear her head for a few hours.

"Sounds like a plan. What time?"

"You know me, I've been ready for hours." She chuckled. "Nia was finishing getting dressed and I'm going to pick her up. Then we can swing by and get you."

"I should be ready in about a half hour. That good?"

"We'll be there. Casual dress. I have on jeans and flip flops."

Yeah, Savannah knew what Dani meant by jeans and flip flops. Like Claudia, everything on Dani's body was high-end designer. As a fashion photographer for several leading women's magazines, Dani stayed on the cutting edge of style. "Right up my alley.

See you guys in a few."

Savannah hung up, feeling momentarily better. She got off the bed and went to her closet to find something equally casual to wear.

Blake barely turned his eyes in her direction when she emerged from the bedroom in concert with the ringing of the doorbell.

"Somebody's at the door honey," he called out absently.

Savannah just shook her head and went to open the door. "Hey, Dani, wanna come in for a minute?"

They kissed cheeks.

"Just a sec to say hello to my favorite married man. Nia is in the car, we're double-parked."

As promised, Danielle was casual, at least in her mind. Her hip-hugging black Versace jeans were encrusted with what looked like cubic zirconia studs along the outside seams. A lavish silver chain belt hung from her waist and shimmied erotically each time she moved. Her petite size-seven feet were tucked into an exquisite pair of red Jimmy Choo sandals with a two-inch heel. Topping it all off was a single button, pristine white midriff blouse with elbow length sleeves. Her inky black hair that flowed almost to her hips when let loose and free was tossed on top of her head in a jazzy attempt at looking slightly disheveled and devilishly sexy.

Dani swept her sunglasses off the bridge of her nose with a flourish and sashayed inside. She struck a pose in front of Blake blocking his view of the game.

"Didn't your good southern mama teach you any manners?" she chastised.

"Yes, never to hit a woman even if she is blocking the game." Blake tried to push her aside and failed. "Come on, Dani, this is the top of the fourth. Mets at bat."

"You mean, you actually recognized me and I don't have on a sport's uniform? I'm impressed." She swatted his arm. "Say hello."

"Hello, Dani," he barked. "You're going to force me to sit up and loose my position on the couch if you don't get out of the way," he practically whined trying to see around her.

Savannah marched over and grabbed Dani by the hand. "It's useless, sis. I could walk in front of him butt naked and he wouldn't notice." She pulled her toward the door. "See you later, baby. Going out with the girls."

He mumbled something unintelligible.

Savannah picked up her mango-colored

Kate Spade purse — which matched her open-toed sandals — from the table in the foyer. "By the time he realizes I'm gone, I'll be back already," she said with a laugh of acceptance. "Come on, let's go."

"I'm determined to break that hypnotic stare one of these days," Danielle said, emphasizing the last four words.

"Good luck." Savannah shut the door behind them.

"Love that bag, by the way," Dani said with a hint of envy in her voice.

"Thanks. And no, you can't borrow it."

Dani huffed in mock offense.

They stepped out into the very warm June afternoon and down the concrete steps of Savannah and Blake's three-story town house, located in Harlem's historic Sugar Hill.

The house was originally owned by Savannah's great-grandparents, who turned it over to Claudia's mother, Sylvia, when she married and then Sylvia passed it on to Claudia on her wedding day and Claudia turned it over to Savannah as a wedding gift to her and Blake just as it had been done in the family for generations. Hopefully, one day Savannah would be able to turn the grand home over to her son or daughter. The family rumor was that Great-

Granddad Jessie won the house in a high-stakes poker game from an old white land baron who figured he'd finally gotten rid of an albatross. It was no more than a rotting shell when Great-Granddad won it, but he and his four brothers worked on it for three solid years until they restored it to its former glory. It had been in the family ever since. A house that was once not worth the time it took to walk past it was now valued at more than one million dollars.

Nia waved as the duo came down the steps toward Dani's brand-new Ford Edge.

Savannah stood for a moment in front of the spanking new SUV with a hand on her hip. She snapped her head toward Dani who had a big smug smirk on her perfectly made-up face.

"So whatcha think?"

"Girl —" Savannah walked around it slowly "— when did you get this?"

"Picked it up yesterday from the dealer. Hop in."

"That little camera thing you do is really paying off," Savannah teased, and got inside the plush vehicle. Dani's job as a fashion photographer for all of the elite magazines afforded her many luxuries; invitations to all the major events and premieres inside and out of the country along with meeting folks that the average person only reads about in the tabloids. She couldn't count the "A list" of stars and socialites who'd become friends over the years that she had in her Rolodex.

Dani laughed, buckled her seat belt and began pulling out. "Gotta do a little something to pay the bills."

Moments later they sped off and headed for downtown Manhattan. By the time they arrived at the Seaport it was bustling with Sunday afternoon activity. The day was glorious, comfortably warm with a light breeze blowing in off the Hudson River, which thankfully didn't smell like garbage, its usual aroma.

"Let's get our tickets first," Nia suggested, "then get something to eat. The first set is at five."

Nia Turner was the organizer of the trio. As a very well-respected and highly paid event planner for major corporations, she was beyond diligent when it came to scheduling and getting people where they needed to be. It got on Savannah's and Dani's last nerve at times but they still relied on her to pull everything together. As typical of Nia, she had their entire day planned right down to the menu at the restaurant she'd selected for brunch.

"Nia, when in the hell do you have time to do all of this with a full-time job?" Savannah asked as Nia led the way to the ticket booth to pick up the concert tickets.

Nia looked over her narrow shoulder with a puzzled expression on her face. "Time to do what?"

Savannah and Dani stole a glance at each other, shook their heads and kept marching along.

After securing the tickets they headed over to Trio, a new Caribbean restaurant with an outdoor café that Nia had discovered and was aching to try out.

"If this place lives up to its reputation I may put it on my list of recommended locations for my clients," Nia said as they were led to their seats beneath a wide white umbrella.

That was another thing about Nia — even when she wasn't working, she was working. She found some kind of way to tie her job in to darn near everything she did. As a result, the three of them often ate for free, got free spa days, discounts on designer clothes, product samples and they were even able to finagle a trip to the island of St. Kitts as part of Nia's "focus group" for a new resort on the island. All the little perks made Nia's drill-sergeant demeanor all the more bearable. Besides, she really was a sweet-heart.

"Oh, and lunch is on me," Nia announced once they were settled in their seats. "But everyone needs to order something different. I want to get a good cross-sampling of the menu, as well as the service." She snapped her menu open then put on her glasses. Truth be told, Nia was blind as a bat but hated to admit it. She spent a great majority of her time squinting, which gave her a rather sour expression to those who didn't know her. Yet her vanity wouldn't allow her to mar her near perfect face with glasses 24/7. And she was terrified of "sticking anything in my eyes," so contacts were out of the question.

"So what have you ladies been up to?" Dani asked as she perused the menu.

"Up to my eyeballs with work," Savannah said. "But that's not unusual."

"Richard still working you to death?"

"He damn sure tries." She laughed lightly. "But it's cool. I like my job."

Nia lowered her menu and quickly tucked away her glasses before blearily focusing on Savannah. "You are entirely too talented to be someone's assistant for the rest of your life, and too damned smart. You need to take your butt back to school and finish your law degree. Then you could run the show, open your own office and work other people to death."

"She's right, Savannah," Dani chimed in. "I decided a long time ago that I was not cut out to be someone's underling. That's why I have to do my own thing. When I don't feel like working, I don't work."

This was a conversation they had at least once every three months. When she looked at her friends' busy, exciting and carefree lives she often questioned whether or not she'd made all the right choices; from settling down and getting married to settling for a job she could do with her eyes closed. Each time she asked the question the answer was still the same — *yes.* Besides, she had what neither of them had — a loving husband and a *secret life.* Inwardly she smiled.

"Enough about me," Savannah said before they got on a roll that would last through brunch. "What have you two been up to?"

Dani and Nia alternated with stories about their latest clients while Savannah tried to concentrate on the nonstop chatter, saying all the appropriate "Mmm, hmms" at all the right places and laughing on cue. But her mind was elsewhere. She had what the girls would call a DDD — *a damned difficult dilemma.* Under normal circumstances she would happily spill her tale all over the white linen tablecloth and listen with amazement as Dani and Nia put their personal spin on what she needed to do. More often than not they were on point. This time as much as she needed their savvy wisdom, she couldn't risk it.

As Nia predicted, the food was incredible. The service was top-notch and Nia had penciled Trio in as a restaurant to recommend. Of course, before they could leave, Nia gained introductions to the owner and manager.

"You did good," Savannah said to Nia as they made their way to the boat.

Nia grinned, flashing a dimple beneath her right eye. "Gotta keep my contacts fresh. My clients only expect the best." Nia linked her arm through Savannah's. "How's the 'family planning' going?" she asked in a soft voice.

Savannah's expression mirrored her internal disappointment. "So far, no good," she said. "But we'll keep trying."

"It will happen when the time is right."

Savannah tilted her head and rested it momentarily on Nia's shoulder. "I hope so. That's the only thing missing in our marriage."

"What's the only thing missing in your

marriage?" Dani cut in with her supersonic hearing.

"A baby," Savannah said.

"It ain't all it's cracked up to be. Just think, if you had a baby, you'd be home changing Pampers instead of hanging with your girls."

"That much is true," Nia conceded. "And what about furthering your career? A baby would definitely put a damper on that."

Savannah drew in a long breath. "I could always go back to school. It would just take longer."

"Hmm," the duo hummed in unison.

"Listen, sis, if it's for you and Blake it will happen and as much as I detest stinky diapers I'd be in your corner, girl. You know that," Dani said.

"Me, too," Nia said, giving Savannah a squeeze.

Savannah smiled. "Thanks." She knew as tough as they pretended to be about permanent relationships and kids, they were true softies at heart. Beneath all the glitz and glamour of Nia and Dani they were both searching for Mr. Right.

They found the boat and got in line behind the others and spent the next two hours relaxing on lounge chairs, sipping frozen margaritas and listening to music.

Savannah tried to stay focused on the music and the lulling pull of the ocean beneath them, but her mind kept going back to her assignment and what it would mean. The results could be devastating. Although she was certain that her husband would never involve himself in anything illegal or underhanded, that wouldn't eliminate him from falling under the murky shadow of suspicion. There was a part of her that seriously considered turning down the assignment. But that, too, had repercussions. If she declined, she was sure that she'd never get another chance and she'd worked damned hard. Worst, the assignment would be given to someone else that wouldn't have the same concerns that she did regarding Blake.

Savannah jumped when she felt her shoulder being shaken. She snapped her head toward Dani. "What?"

"I was talking to you and you weren't paying me a bit of attention. The music is cool but it ain't that good."

Savannah looked around and realized that the concert was over and people were starting to leave. She blinked to clear her head and reached for her purse.

"To be truthful, you haven't been yourself all day," Nia said as they began heading out.

"You've been totally distracted. What's up? It's not the baby thing, is it?"

Savannah took a deep breath. She knew that she couldn't reveal all of the details but maybe she could offer some "scenarios" to her friends and get their take on it.

"Just struggling with a case that I've been working on," she began.

"What about it?" Dani asked.

They strolled along the boardwalk to the parking area.

Savannah cleared her throat. "Well, uh, we've been working on a case . . . a husband and wife thing. Uh, divorce. And, well, the wife is our client and the husband claims he has no assets. But the wife believes that he does and wants us to uncover his assets that she feels she's entitled to."

Dani shrugged. "So what's the big deal? Happens every day. Bastard probably is hiding his net worth so he can keep the mother lode for himself."

"The conflict is that I know the husband." Her heart knocked in her chest.

Nia stopped in her tracks and squinted at Savannah. "You do?"

"Did you tell your boss, Richard whatshisname?" Dani asked.

Savannah shook her head. "This is a big assignment for me. Most of the time I simply do research, prepare briefs, schedule appointments, things like that. Richard is trusting me to take care of this on my own."

"So how well do you *know* the husband?" Nia asked. "Better yet, do we know him?" She shot a look at Dani who cocked a brow in anticipation.

Savannah did a rapid analysis of how long she'd known both women, where they'd gone to school, the neighborhoods they'd grown up in and the friends they had in common. It was a safe bet to say that she knew "the husband" from the one neighborhood they did not share in common. "I actually met him during high school when I would spend part of my summer with my aunt in New Jersey."

"You two didn't have 'a thing' did you?" Dani wanted to know.

Savannah shook her head. "No. It was nothing like that. He lived on the block, that's all."

Nia squinted. "I really don't see the problem. Unless you kept in touch over all those years, you don't really know him anymore, know what I mean?"

"I guess . . ." Savannah mumbled. "I suppose what I'm asking is what would either of you do, if you got an assignment to investigate an acquaintance — and that

74

investigation could lead to something ugly for the person that you know?"

Dani disengaged the alarm and door lock on her SUV and the ladies got in. Dani slipped on her sunglasses. "Me, if it was a distant acquaintance like this guy and my job hinged on it, I'd do my job. If he's innocent it will all come out anyway."

"I agree. It's not like he's your best buddy or something."

But he is my best buddy, Savannah thought. *Her husband.* However as Nia said, if everything is on the up and up it won't be a problem. *If.* What if it wasn't?

CHAPTER 7

When Savannah arrived back home she was no closer to having an answer for her DDD than before she left. Unfortunately, she would have to make a decision and quickly. Time was of the essence.

"Hey, babe," Blake called out.

Savannah dropped her purse and keys on the hall table and followed the sound of his voice. For a moment she stood in the doorway of the kitchen observing the man she loved. A sense of warmth and peace filled her as she watched him check the chicken he'd put in the oven. What tickled her most was his attire. He had on his black-and-white barbecue apron that hung from his neck and reached his knees and nothing else.

She couldn't help but smile. Some men wouldn't think twice about fixing a meal, especially Sunday dinner. But not Blake. He loved — among many things — cooking for his wife. He was adamant about fairness and balance and saw no reason why two people who worked equally as hard shouldn't share the responsibility of managing a home. He was like that about his work, as well. He treated others as he wanted to be treated. She'd known him to turn down lucrative deals because he didn't like the way an employer treated his employees. And that's when she made her decision. She knew her husband as well she knew herself. Blake would be the last one to become involved in something that may ultimately prove to be unjust to someone else.

"Don't get those buns of yours too close to the oven," she said, her entry line full of innuendo. She crossed the threshold of the kitchen with a wanton smile on her face.

Blake closed the oven door and slowly turned to his wife. His eyes darkened with intent. He tossed the oven mitt on the counter. "But I always thought you liked my buns warm and toasty."

They walked toward each other as if on cue. She stood before him and looked up into his eyes. "I love you," she said from the depths of her heart, and wrapped her arms lightly around his waist.

For a moment he looked at her with a question hovering in his eyes, but then it was gone. "Right back at ya." He leaned down and kissed her slow and deep then pulled back. "So how was the day with the girls?"

"Great. We did one of those afternoon jazz boat rides, had brunch at this really cool place, Trio — we'll have to try it." She leaned her hip against the counter. "Sure smells good in here. What are we having?"

"Chef's surprise. I'm trying out a new chicken recipe."

Savannah chuckled. "You and your recipes." She looked him up and down. "Uh, do I dress up or down for dinner?"

"My preference would be nothing at all, but I'll give you a break on this one." He winked.

"Can I help with anything?"

"Nope, got it all covered. About another twenty minutes for the bird and we can eat."

"Great. I'm going to change."

She walked off into the bedroom kicked off her shoes and got undressed. Since Blake had opted for an apron as his attire, she figured she'd up the ante a bit and give him a bit of Victoria's Secret to go with dessert. She giggled as she hunted through her lingerie drawer to find the perfect scanty outfit.

Just as she was slipping into her peach-colored thong, the phone rang. *Blake must have answered,* she realized when it only rang twice. Probably one of his buddies who'd bet on the baseball game earlier, she thought as she adjusted her demibra.

The bedroom door eased open.

"Phone," Blake said sticking his head in.

Savannah turned to give him an eyeful. She posed provocatively. "Who is it?"

Blake lost his train of thought when he feasted his eyes on her. He cleared his throat. "Umm, someone named Jean from your TLC group." He stuck the phone out in front of him.

Her heart jammed somewhere in her throat and she had to suck in air through widened nostrils. "Oh, thanks. Must be about my order."

She took the phone from him, gave him a "see you later" smile while holding the phone in the valley of her breasts waiting for him to leave. He took a step toward her and she wagged her finger *no.*

Pouting like a little boy Blake reluctantly backed out the door. "What's so top secret about some old body scrub anyway?" he grumbled.

Savannah waited until he was out of earshot. "Hello?"

"Hi, Savannah, is this a bad time?"

"No, not at all. We were getting ready for dinner. Is everything okay?"

"I'm doing my basic follow up that I conduct with all of the Cartel members when they get their first assignment."

"Oh." She didn't know what else to say.

"Did you read the contents?"

"Yes, I did."

"Any questions?"

"No, everything is very clear."

"Excellent. So you will be taking on the assignment?" It was more of a statement than a question.

She glanced toward the partially opened door. This was her chance to back out, stick this in someone else's hands. But she'd never backed away from a challenge. Never.

"Absolutely."

"Wonderful. If you need anything we're here to assist you. Expect your package in the next day or so. Good luck, Savannah."

Before Savannah had a chance to respond the call was disconnected. In the recesses of her mind she heard the theme music to *Mission Impossible* playing and almost laughed. Almost.

As Savannah rested in the arms of her husband later that night she wondered what she would do if she discovered that Blake was doing something wrong. She pressed closer to the warmth of his body as a slight chill ran through her.

"I'm heading to court, Savannah," Richard said, stopping for a hot minute at her desk.

Savannah glanced up at him over the rim of her reading glasses. "You look harried and your tie is crooked." She stood and adjusted his tie.

"This is a big case. If we win it will be a major coup for the company."

"You'll do fine. You're totally prepared."

"I can't thank you enough for staying on Friday. But I couldn't have gotten it all together without you. I hope I didn't completely ruin your plans."

"Not at all. Everything worked out fine. Fortunately for you I have a very understanding husband." She tucked the hem of his tie inside his navy blue suit jacket. "Now you look like a winner." She grinned.

"Thanks. Wish me luck," he said, hurrying off.

"Luck!" she called out. Just as she sat back down, Jeremy from the mail room approached with the mail cart.

"Hey, Jeremy. How was your weekend?"

Jeremy was a college student that worked part-time at the office to help pay his tuition, and he was always full of stories about his college partying antics, which always brought back memories of her own wild college days at Spelman University.

"Pretty quiet this weekend, Mrs. Fields. Had to study." He grimaced. "Exams next week." He began piling the day's mail in her inbox.

"Still planning on going to law school?"

"Yep. That's the plan." He took a plain brown box out of the cart and set it down on her desk. "This one is for you. Kinda heavy."

She pulled it toward her and immediately knew what it was before even looking at it.

"Came by messenger." He paused, waited for a response and when he didn't get one he added, "I signed for it," in a way that hedged for information.

Savannah looked up at him and gave him a short smile. "Thanks." Unfortunately for Jeremy she wasn't giving up the goods.

Realizing that a "thanks" was all he was going to get, he said his goodbyes and pushed off to the next office.

Savannah stared at the box for several moments. She'd seen the same kind of box delivered to her mother's door on several occasions. In the beginning Savannah always thought that her mother must be doing a booming bath and body product business. Humph, she'd sure been fooled.

She also knew that her own box would contain the tools she would need to pull off her investigation; everything from listening devices, fingerprinting equipment, burglary tools to handguns if necessary. Every member of the Cartel, upon completion of training, was issued a permit to carry a weapon. She hoped she'd never have cause to use it, but it was good to know it was at her disposal. Her fingers itched to open the box and see what goodies were inside, but it would have to wait. She'd have to compare each item with the TLC catalog to determine which bath and body products were masquerading as something else. She kept the catalog tucked away at home.

In the meantime she'd keep herself occupied by researching as much information as she could on her target. But to ensure that her snooping was never traced back to her office computer, she'd use the computers at the library during her lunch break.

Savannah glanced at her watch. It was only ten thirty. She felt an early lunch coming on. She couldn't wait to see what she could uncover on Ms. Tristan Montgomery.

CHAPTER 8

"Ms. Montgomery, Mr. Fletcher is on the phone," her secretary said into the intercom.

Tristan grimaced. She really didn't have the time or the inclination to deal with Morris Fletcher. He rubbed her the wrong way. Not only had he tried to hit on her, he was always telling her what to do with her money. It was hers, wasn't it? Didn't her father leave everything to her? She could do what she damn-well pleased. And if it wasn't for those hateful Board of Directors and the obnoxious Mr. Fletcher, she could do as she pleased.

"Thank you, Cindy." At least that's what she thought her name was. She'd completely lost count of the array of secretaries that swung in and out of her door. She expected a lot from her staff and if you couldn't cut it, you were out. Simple.

She pressed down the flashing red light, drew in a breath and blew out a bored,

"Hello."

"Tristan, we need to talk."

"About what now?"

"The development project of course."

She rolled her eyes. "What's the problem this time?"

"I need to present a financial report to the Board at the end of the month and I need to go over some figures with you."

"Fine. Can you be here in an hour? If not we will have to make it another time. My schedule is very tight today." She had a hair and nail appointment and one with her masseuse. Then she needed to dart over to her designer and see if her outfit was ready for Friday night. She wanted to look extra special for Blake, whether or not he brought his frumpy — at least that's what she imagined — wife.

"An hour is pretty tight, Tristan, but I'll be there."

"Good." She hung up the phone without another word.

Tristan leaned back in her imported red-leather high-backed chair and swiveled it until she faced the panoramic window that looked out onto the skyline of Manhattan.

Everyone thought she was no more than a spoiled, airheaded woman who would never be anywhere had it not been for her father and his money. She smiled slowly. They had no idea who they were dealing with. Tristan Montgomery may be a lot of things, but stupid and naive were not on her list of attributes. Playing the dumb, over-sexed heiress suited her purposes fine. Her father, God rest his soul, taught her well and she lived by his words: "Never let them see your true hand and, above all, trust no one."

Her eyes tightened ever so slightly as she gazed outward onto a world that she could write her own check for.

She reached for the phone and dialed the private number. It rang three times before the familiar voice answered.

"Buy ten more," she said, then hung up the phone. She lifted her chin defiantly. No, Tristan Montgomery was no fool.

Savannah juggled the box, her purse, tote and a shopping bag of groceries as she tried to get her front door open. To top it off she was dripping wet, unable to manage her load and hold up an umbrella as she'd darted down the street from her car to her town house.

She finally got the door open and shoved it closed with her hip. Her purse and tote landed on the hall table before she went to the kitchen to deposit the groceries.

It was barely five o'clock. Richard was feeling generous after a good day in court and sent everyone home early. Perfect for her. She knew Blake wouldn't be home before seven, which would give her plenty of time to go over the information she'd gotten at the library, review the catalog and her products and still have dinner ready by the time hubby walked through the door.

Quickly she got out of her wet clothes and changed into a tank top and a pair of buttersoft sweatpants. Then went to the kitchen to season two steaks and put them in the oven.

Once that was out of the way, she headed to the bedroom, sat down on the side of the bed and opened the box. Inside was the standard pink carryall case. With a bit of apprehensive excitement she flipped the faux gold latch and lifted the lid.

Everything looked innocent enough — at least to those who didn't know better. She lifted the two ounce bottle of body oil which, when opened, was actually a tranquilizer, along with the matching bottle of bubble bath. Of course, one had to be careful with the latter as you didn't want your suspect to drown in the tub.

Savannah got up from the side of the bed and crossed the room to her dresser. She opened the bottom drawer and fished out the folder containing the TLC catalog tucked beneath her sweaters. She brought it back to the bed and flipped it open.

She picked up the silver cylindrical tube from the case then scanned the pages of the catalog until she found the matching image with a description. She screwed off the top and emptied the contents out on the bed — burglary tools. There were picks for a variety of locks, putty to make key impressions and a small case to seal the putty. She returned the items to the tube. In what appeared to be a makeup case, beneath the pressed powder were several black flat disks. When adhered to any surface, they would serve as tracking devices that could be picked up on the GPS system of her cell phone and her car. The smaller disks were listening devices that could be placed inconspicuously just about anywhere that conversation took place. The case that contained the blush had a secret compartment, as well. When the blush was lifted out of its well, there was a tiny circular piece of metal.

Savannah flipped through the catalog to be sure it was what she thought. This was actually an upgraded listening and recording device that could be inserted in a telephone. She smiled.

In a separate compartment was her toss away cell phone. She already had her digital camera with a powerful zoom lens, small enough to tuck away in a pocket.

There was also a bottle of spray perfume that was actually mace, as well as dusting power that was used to dust for fingerprints along with its own dual-purpose makeup brush.

She expertly assembled a gun from the inconspicuous metal pieces in the case. She lifted the .22 in her palm, raised it and pointed. Satisfied, she returned all the items to their compartments, closed the case and locked it, returned the catalog to the bottom drawer and went to start dinner. By the time she had all four burners going on the stove and steak grilling in the oven, the front door opened and slammed shut.

Savannah grinned as she stirred the pot of mixed vegetables. Her man was home. Maybe tonight she could interest her hubby in a game of poker. Strip, of course, and of course she intended to lose each hand. It made Blake feel like he was invincible and it made her feel totally wicked.

Blake hung up his tan trench coat in the hall closet and set his briefcase inside then shut the door. He dropped a copy of the

Wall Street Journal on top of the table. Sounds and scents came from the kitchen, but he hesitated before going to greet his wife. He glanced at the headline in the sidebar then on the front page of the paper. *Montgomery Enterprise Inks Historic Deal with Blake Fields, Architects, PPC.*

He should be elated. His name and his company was showcased in one of the most elite papers in the country. It was what happened after the paper hit the newsstands that disturbed him. He'd handled it as best he could. At least he thought he did. It was getting sticky and so much rode on every piece of the puzzle fitting perfectly. And his conscience was the piece that just wouldn't seem to fit.

"Blake, is that you?" Savannah called out from the kitchen.

He heard her soft footsteps approach and drew himself up, putting on his game face. "Hey, babe," he said as she came from the kitchen to where he stood.

A warm smile lit up her eyes, and his heart knocked hard in his chest. Blake loved Savannah with all his heart. He'd do everything within his power not to hurt her.

She walked up to him and lifted her head for a kiss. Blake took her in his arms, kissed her lips, the tip of her nose and her eyelids, then held her close. He shut his eyes and chanted deep in his heart how much she meant to him.

Savannah eased back and tilted her head up to look at him. A soft frown creased between her brows. She stroked his cheek compelling him to look at her.

"What is it?" she gently asked, reading him like an old family recipe.

He ran his hand slowly up and down the gentle sway of her back.

"Nothing, baby, just tired." The right corner of his mouth curved slightly upward. He brushed a wisp of hair away from her forehead. "How was your day?" He put his arm around her shoulders as they walked into the living room.

"The usual hustle and bustle. Richard did well in court today so he let the troops off early." At least that much of her day was true, she thought.

"I'm sure he owes his courtroom success to you as always." He plopped down onto the couch, stretched his legs out in front of him and loosened his burgundy colored tie.

Savannah sat opposite him, braced her arms on her thighs and leaned forward. "Do you think I'm wasting my time and talents at the firm?"

Blake drew in a slow breath. "I don't think

you're wasting your time, but I do think you've grown comfortable. You can do that job with your eyes closed. You have a thirst for law and all things legal. I know you would whiz through law school if you decided it was what you wanted to do. But you have to want to do it."

Savannah was quiet for a moment. Being an attorney had been her dream since she was a teen and served on the debate and tort teams in high school. She had loved participating in mock trials. In all the years that she'd been on the team in high school and then college, she'd only lost one case as a defense attorney. But then she met Blake and her dreams for preparing her opening and closing remarks took a backseat to being a wife and one day mother.

She loved her job. Sure, she knew she could run rings around both of the partners if she set her mind to it. But if she went back to law school and then took the bar, her biological clock would barely be ticking. Besides she wouldn't be very threatening in the court room with a big belly and a "glow."

"Why are you asking this now? Or should I say again?" Blake asked.

"I've been thinking about it more, I guess. And Nia and Dani swear I'm wasting my time as a paralegal being worked to death."

A faint smile dusted her face. "And if I went back to school, got my law degree and passed the bar, I could hang out my own shingle."

"You could. Is that what you want?"

Savannah got up and came to sit next to him. "You know what I want," she said, her voice laced with fleeting hope.

Blake pulled her close. "If it's going to happen it will, baby." He kissed the top of her head. "Stop worrying."

Savannah pressed her head against Blake's chest and drew in a long slow breath. Her heart jumped. She could swear under oath that she smelled perfume on his shirt.

CHAPTER 9

Savannah stood in front of her island counter, staring at the trays of food. She couldn't seem to move. For the last few minutes, since Blake had excused himself to take an early shower, she felt as if she were moving in slow motion.

She kept telling herself that she was simply imagining things, that her mind was in overdrive because of her assignment and Blake's possible involvement. Yet, her heart said something totally different.

How close do you have to be to someone to get their scent all over you? Her instincts went on alert when she greeted him in the hallway. It was not so much that he held her — something that he always did — it was the *way* he held her.

No! Just stop it. She trusted her husband. He'd never given her a reason not to.

"Earth to Savannah."

She jumped and looked toward the archway of the kitchen. Blake was grinning at her and running a towel over his damp air. His chest was bare and chiseled, his loose-fitting drawstring pajama bottoms hanging low on his hips. He came toward her and she felt her clit twitch the way it always did whenever he looked at her like that — whenever *he* looked like that.

Savannah swallowed back the doubt, pushed the impossible thoughts out of her head and walked toward her husband. She draped her arms around his neck and entwined her fingers.

"Ready to eat?"

"That's a loaded question." He ran his warm lips along the column of her neck.

Savannah shivered with delight. Her eyes drifted shut while she pressed closer to Blake. The clean scent of soap and water wafted beneath her nose. Her senses jerked and her earlier doubts rushed to the surface.

"Why don't we put everything on trays and take it into the bedroom?" Blake suggested.

Savannah swallowed and pulled in a slow breath. "Sure." She stepped out of his arms. "Wanna get out the trays?" She moved away.

"Savannah, is something wrong?" He put his hand on her shoulder and turned her around. She looked everywhere but in his eyes. "You've been acting kinda weird since I came home."

Her gaze bumped against his. "I smelled perfume on your shirt," she blurted out.

He sputtered a nervous laugh. "Perfume?"

She folded her arms and stared at her husband — waiting.

The afternoon flashed through his head in a nanosecond. He couldn't explain. He didn't understand it himself.

"You're kidding, right?" was his comeback. "How in the world would perfume get on my shirt?"

"That's what I want to know."

Blake slowly shook his head in denial. "I think Richard is working you too hard and your imagination is getting the best of you." He stepped up to her and lifted her chin so that he could look right into her eyes. "The only woman I let get that close to me is you." His gaze danced over her face before settling on her eyes. "Only you," he said softly. He pulled her to him. "Come here." He held her tightly. "I love you, Savannah, only you." He pressed his face into her hair, felt her heart pound against his chest. He shut his eyes and said a silent prayer that the events of the day would stay buried and not rear their ugly head. He didn't know what he would do with his life if Savannah were hurt by his stupidity. He wouldn't let that happen. That's all there was to it.

Blake stepped back, holding Savannah at arm's length. He put a smile on his face. "So, we're good?"

She nodded.

"No more imagining things?"

She pushed out a laugh. "I guess I was being silly."

"You . . . never." He kissed the top of her head. "I'm starved." He turned away and walked across the kitchen to the cabinets and took out two lap trays and the dishes.

They worked side by side filling their plates.

"How about some wine with dinner?" Blake suggested.

"Sure. I'll get it."

"And I'll get us all set up." He took the two trays, balancing them like an experienced waiter and walked into the bedroom.

Savannah sighed heavily as she watched him walk away. She knew her husband loved her. But that never stopped a man from straying. She also knew if she kept dwelling on it, things would turn ugly. He'd never given her a reason not to trust him and she wasn't going to start losing faith in her man or her marriage now.

Savannah went to the cabinet and took

out a bottle of merlot, then filled the ice bucket with ice and stuck the bottle inside. She drew in a long breath of resolve. Blake and Savannah forever, she reminded herself and headed to the bedroom to join her husband.

Blake had dimmed the lights, lit scented candles and turned down the bed. He'd popped a Kem CD in the player and *their* song, "Love Calls," was on. They'd played the *Kemistry* CD so many times that the original had worn out and they'd had to buy another one.

Savannah smiled. "Now, this is what I call intimate dining." She crossed the room and set the ice bucket down on the nightstand. She pulled her top up and over her head and tossed it to the side. Her pants came next. Her body warmed when she saw Blake's eyes darken with lust.

"You are so incredibly beautiful. More so than when I married you."

She stepped up to him. "Do you really mean that?"

"Every word." He kissed her lips then ran his tongue lightly along the contour of her mouth. "Hmm," he hummed deep in his throat. He snaked his arm around her bare waist and pulled her flush against him.

Savannah felt his erection press against

her stomach. Her heart thundered.

"If we keep this up we'll never get through dinner," she whispered against his mouth.

"You're probably right." He ran his fingers along her spine before releasing her.

The settled themselves on the bed, relaxing against the overstuffed pillows, listening to music while making light conversation.

"Did I tell you that we've been invited to a dinner party on Friday night?"

Savannah chewed thoughtfully on her succulent steak, the seasoned juices flowing over her lips and tongue. "Yeah, I think so. What time?"

"Eight."

"I'll make sure that Richard doesn't pull one of his traumas so that I can get out of the office early. Is this a dressy thing?"

"I have no idea. You're the fashionista in the fam, so you'll have to decide on outfits."

Savannah giggled. As quiet as it was kept, her very successful businessman husband, who looked like a cover model when he put on clothes, actually hated to get dressed up. He was most comfortable in a pair of jeans, an old white T-shirt and bare feet. Blake attributed it all to his early years of growing up on the West Coast in L.A. and spending his days and nights on the beach. She took pleasure in shopping for him and putting his outfits together. Blake had no idea how a patterned tie could go with a pinstriped shirt or why red and burgundy spelled power or that he could never have enough starched white shirts.

"I'll take care of it," she said. She lifted her tray from her lap and put it on the nightstand next to her side of the bed then wiped her mouth with the cloth napkin. "Want some more wine?"

"Sure." He held up his glass while she poured.

"So tell me, how is it working with Tristan Montgomery?"

A line of wine spilled over his lips and dribbled down his chin. Savannah grabbed a napkin and wiped the spill.

"Maybe I didn't need more wine," he said, sputtering a laugh while dabbing at his chest with the napkin.

That bad feeling snaked through her again. She glanced at Blake but he didn't meet her gaze. He set his glass down.

"She's your typical spoiled princess," he said with a slight shrug. "Wants everything her way and now."

"Oh," was all she could say.

"Why do you ask?"

"Just wondering, that's all. I've seen her face in the papers and magazines, mostly gossip columns. She's really quite beautiful."

"Hmm."

"I guess I'll see for myself on Friday, huh?"

"Yeah . . . you will." He reached for his glass of wine and took a long slow sip. He wasn't looking forward to Friday, but there was no way he could get out of it.

CHAPTER 10

"You what?" Nia squealed into the phone.

"Yes, perfume," Savannah said in a hushed voice.

"Aw, hell naw, not Blake. Girl, are you sure?"

Savannah frowned. "Pretty sure."

"Being pretty sure isn't enough to start thinking your man is cheating on you. What did he say when you asked him about it, 'cause I know you did."

"He denied it, said I must be overworked, stuff like that."

"And why don't you believe him?"

Savannah sighed heavily. "He . . . just the way he was acting."

"Acting like how? Guilty?"

"No, not exactly." She shook her head. "I can't put it into words. All I can say is that I had a bad feeling and that there was something he wasn't telling me."

"Savannah, that man loves the ground you

walk on. I've known Blake for a while and I've seen the way he looks at you when you aren't looking. He loves you, girl."

Savannah's eyes filled. She sniffed hard. "I know," she said, her voice wobbling. "I'm just being silly. Maybe it's PMS or something."

"Probably so. You know how hormones can make you half crazy." She chuckled. "So don't go getting yourself all twisted in a knot, okay? Go eat some chocolate. It always works for me."

Savannah sniffed and chuckled. "Okay. Look, I gotta go. Thanks for listening."

"Anytime. That's what friends are for. Talk to you later in the week. And I definitely want all the details from the little gathering at Ms. Montgomery's."

"Will do. 'Bye."

Savannah slowly hung up the phone. Nia was right. She dabbed at her eyes with a tissue from the box on her desk. She needed to let it go and trust her husband. And she would.

Blake sat at his drafting table working on some sketches for a possible job renovating an abandoned hospital into affordable housing units. The space was of course, mammoth, but it would take some real creative genius to rid the environment of what it once was.

He started to toss his tie over his shoulder and out of the way as he always did when he was at work and sketching, when he realized that, much to Savannah's chagrin and his delight, it was a jeans and T-shirt day for him. He grinned. He had no outside meetings and was not expecting any clients to visit. He was free! He adjusted his banker's lamp and started to whistle as he looked at the hospital specs and began formulating a design.

Blake worked steadily for about an hour, the visions in his mind coming to life on his sketch pad. An old tune by Miles Davis wailed softly in the background. He was in his element. This is what he lived for — creating, making people's dreams come true.

A knot suddenly formed in his gut. Everyone except for Savannah. He straightened. His gaze danced around the room, bouncing off his desk, his wall of honors, his tools of the trade. He knew how desperately Savannah wanted a child and so did he. But the fates seemed to be against them. Savannah would make an incredible mother, he knew that. And it killed him every month when he saw the look of hurt and disappointment in her eyes. They'd purchased so many pregnancy kits that they could own stock.

He sighed heavily and put down his drafting pen. He succeeded in every other area of his life except the one that mattered most. It had been six years with no luck. Maybe they should consider adopting, he thought, but knew that Savannah would feel even more like a failure if he brought it up. It was the one area of their otherwise idyllic lives that was left unfulfilled and he had no idea what to do about it.

All of the doctors and specialists they'd seen had concurred that they were both healthy and they could find no cause as to why they could not conceive. Be patient they all said. Be patient. But he knew as well as Savannah that the clock was ticking.

The ringing of his phone tugged him away from the turn of his thoughts. He pulled himself up from the stool and went to his desk.

"Yes," he said, pressing down on the flashing intercom light.

"Ms. Montgomery is on line two," Jasmine said.

"Tell her I'm busy in a meeting."

"I did. She insists on speaking with you. She said it's urgent."

Blake pushed out a breath of annoyance as their last encounter flashed through his head. "Fine. I'll take it."

He plunked down in his chair behind his desk, took a moment to compose himself then snatched up the phone.

"Yes, Ms. Montgomery, what can I do for you?"

Her tinkling laughter ran through the line. "Blake, I was sure we'd gotten to first base — or at least a first-name basis. Ms. Montgomery sounds so old. And after the other day . . ."

Blake cleared his throat. "Tristan, what can I do for you?"

"That's so much better, don't you think?" She didn't wait for a response. "I'm in your area and it's nearly lunchtime. I'd like you to meet me at the Bistro in say twenty minutes."

"I'm really busy. I hadn't planned on going out for lunch. As a matter of fact, Jasmine just ordered my lunch from the deli downstairs."

"Tell her to eat it. I'll be there in twenty. I do hope to see you there, Blake." She hung up before he could blink.

"Dammit!" He slammed down the phone and ran his hand roughly over his face. This was the last thing he needed. Tristan was getting totally out of hand and he was at a serious crossroads as to what to do about it. The one thing he had done about it so far was lie to his wife.

Savannah had been right when she said she smelled perfume on his shirt. His heart nearly stopped when she said it. But he should have known that Tristan would find a way to leave her mark.

Once again, she'd come to the office unexpected. Jasmine was out to lunch and the front office was open game for Tristan. She actually came into his office without knocking, catching him completely off guard.

"Blake, I hope you don't mind that I just barged in. There was no one out front," she'd said, her version of an apology. She shut the door behind her.

Blake sat upright in his chair. "Come in. What can I do for you today? We didn't have a meeting scheduled."

"No. Just an impromptu visit." She slinked across the room until she reached his desk. She sat on its edge, her tight skirt hiking up nearly to her hips.

Blake swallowed as he tore his gaze away from the buttery smooth thigh. She crossed her legs at the knee, and Blake swore he caught of glimpse of something hot pink.

Tristan leaned over, displaying a teasing view of cleavage as she adjusted his tie and before he knew what was happening, she kissed him. Her tongue was in his mouth and her fingers gripped his neck, holding him in place.

It could have been a second but it seemed to last an eternity before he gained enough of his senses to peel her away.

He wiped his mouth with the back of his hand. Her fire-red lipstick imprinted itself. He pushed back from his seat. Her eyes gleamed. She ran her tongue across her lips in a slow, sensual dance.

"Just as I thought," she said, her voice thick and vibrating. "Sweet and experienced."

"You need to leave. Now."

She hopped down from the edge of his desk and walked right up to him. Her breasts pressed hard up against his chest. He could see the flecks of light brown in her eyes. Her breath was hot and sweet.

Tristan took his hands and wrapped them around her waist. She pressed her pelvis up against him.

"I want you, Blake Fields. And it's my intention to have you. One way or the other."

She stepped back, let the heat of her eyes

run a stream of fire up and down his body.

"This isn't going to work. I'll have my lawyers contact yours about rescinding the contract."

Tristan tossed her head back and laughed. "You mean to tell me you would lose out on the biggest land deal this town has seen in decades simply because a very desirable, beautiful, rich woman wants to go to bed with you?" She laughed again. "Trust me. I may seem like nothing more than a sex-starved socialite, but my lawyers aren't. If you even think about breaking this deal, the only thing you'll be drawing from that moment on are sketches from inside a jail cell for breach of contract and anything else my lawyers can think of. I'll take everything, your house, your business, your sacred marriage. By the time I get finished ripping your life to shreds you'll pray to let me make love to you to take the pain away."

She smiled so sweetly one would have thought she'd just wished him a happy birthday. She picked up her purse from the desk and turned toward the door.

"Think about it," she said, before opening the door and walking out, shutting it softly behind her.

For several moments he stood there in stunned disbelief. She'd essentially blackmailed him. He could still taste her on his lips, in his mouth and feel her hands on his body. What had he gotten himself into? Better yet, how was he going to find a way out without ruining everything he cared about?

All those thoughts ran through his head as he walked the three blocks to Bistro.

When he arrived he spotted her immediately. She was sitting at the outdoor table beneath an umbrella, wide, dark shades shielded her eyes. She took off her glasses when he stood above her.

"What is this about, Tristan?"

"You could say hello."

He jaw clenched. He didn't respond.

"I see we're still a bit testy. Please have a seat while we wait for our table."

Grudgingly, Blake sat down.

Tristan leaned forward, slid her hand beneath the table and placed it on his knee. "Admit it. You enjoyed it as much as I did. What could be more exciting than something forbidden?"

Danielle and her crew were in the van on their way to a photo shoot. They were already late and midtown traffic was horrendous.

"Take the next right, Adam," Dani called out from the backseat. She stared out the passenger window and her heart jumped up into her throat. The van slowed as it moved into the turning lane at the red light. She must be seeing things. "Wait! I need to get out."

"No time for potty breaks. We're already late. I'll have you there in five minutes," Adam said.

Instinct kicked in and she did what she was trained to do — she started shooting. Her high-speed camera snapped in rapid-fire succession.

The van roared off and away.

"What are you getting so snap happy about back there?" Lauren, her lighting assistant, asked.

Dani swallowed. "Nothing. Just testing the equipment." She prayed that it was nothing.

CHAPTER 11

By the time Danielle walked through the doors of her loft apartment in the West Village it was nearing midnight, yet the streets below were still alive with activity. The city that never sleeps, she thought absently. Under normal circumstances she would hop in the shower, wrap herself up in her favorite fluffy robe, sip a glass of white wine and hit the sack. This wasn't normal circumstances.

It had taken all of her concentration to stay focused on the photo shoot. Several times Adam had to get her attention because her thoughts had drifted off to what she'd seen on Amsterdam Avenue — her best friend's husband nestled up with the notorious Tristan Montgomery.

She knew Tristan from way back in the early days of her photography career. She'd started off working freelance for some of the rags, snatching what pictures she could until she finally landed a reputable gig with

Fashion Daily. One of her first assignments had been to attend Fashion Week and not only capture the photos of the supermodels but the fashion aficionados that attended. Tristan Montgomery was front and center. She attended the event with one man but left with another.

There was something about Tristan that totally fascinated Dani. She wasn't sure if it was her incredible beauty, the charisma that she wielded as easily as she took a breath or the fact that she had yet to reach thirty years old and she was one of the wealthiest and most powerful single females in America according to *Forbes* magazine.

Dani began to capture as many images as she could of the striking socialite, from random shopping trips on Fifth Avenue, jogging in Central Park with her Yorkie, to her sunning on her yacht in the Virgin Islands, movie premieres and political dinners. Her portfolio of Tristan Montgomery was thick and eclectic.

She stood in her dark room, the roll of film in her hand. If she developed the roll and her worst fears were true, what would she do? She tossed the roll on the table and returned to her bedroom.

"Are you sure?" Nia asked rubbing her eyes

and yawning simultaneously. She squinted at the illuminated numbers on the digital bedside clock but couldn't quite make them out.

"Dammit, girl, you're the one who can't see! Yes, I'm sure. Do you think I would have gotten you out of your sleep at 2:00 a.m. if I wasn't sure?"

Nia groaned, turned partially on her side and sat up. She turned on the light. She pressed her face close to the neon numbers. Yep, Dani was right. It was 2:00 a.m.

"Okay, okay, I'm awake. Now, tell me what happened again?"

Dani sucked her teeth before proceeding to tell her who and what she'd seen earlier in the day.

Nia sputtered an expletive only fit for sailors.

"My sentiments exactly," Dani said. "So what are you going to do with the pictures?"

"That's why I called you. I'm torn. I mean, I'm Savannah's friend and if she saw my man screwing around with another woman, I would want her to tell me."

"It could be anything, maybe she was wiping lint off his pants." But the longer Nia thought about it the dumber it sounded and the more she was convinced it wasn't the case at all. Especially not after the conversation that she had with Savannah the other day, which she now told Dani about.

For several moments they sat on either end of the phone in silence.

"What are we going to do?" they suddenly said jointly.

A collective breath pushed through the phone lines.

"I don't know," echoed in the morning air.

"I have friends at Bistro," Nia said. "Let me make a call in the morning. See if he made the reservation or if she did."

"How will that help?"

"How should I know? But maybe it will tell us something before we go to Savannah — if we go to Savannah."

The following afternoon during her lunch break, Nia took a cab across town to Bistro, deciding on a personal visit as opposed to a phone call. She smiled and waved at the familiar faces of the staff and headed toward the back office. She knocked lightly on the door.

"Come in," came the slightly accented voice.

Nia opened the door and stepped inside the tight, cramped office of Jean Dubois. He stood with a broad smile on his flat face when he saw her.

"Nia! My favorite customer. Are you here to bring me more business?"

"Actually I'm here for a favor." She explained what she needed.

"Our guest list is private," he said slowly, glancing at her above his half-frame wire-rimmed glasses. "But for you I will make an exception. Can you at least tell me why you need our guest list?"

"It's personal."

He gave a short nod and reached for his phone. "Jules, will you bring me our reservation list from yesterday. Yes, thank you." He hung up the phone.

Moments later Nia was walking out of Bistro with a copy of the reservation list. It didn't take long for her to spot the name she was looking for. She hailed a cab and headed back to her office.

Slowly Nia sat down behind her desk, staring at the list. With a heavy heart she picked up her phone and dialed Dani on her cell.

Dani picked up on the second ring. She listened silently to what Nia had to say. After hanging up there was only one thing she could do. She went to her darkroom.

Now she could add these, she thought, watching the damning photographs materialize in the solution. She took her long tweezers and lifted the wet paper from the tub of chemicals.

A part of her had wanted to be wrong. She wanted to look at the pictures and see how silly she'd been.

Her heart and her hopes sank. Now what was she going to do? What were they going to do?

CHAPTER 12

Savannah left the office early. She wanted to have plenty of time to get ready for the dinner party at Tristan Montgomery's place. More important she wanted to get home long before her husband so that she could be sure to tuck away her tools of the trade that she would need on her assignment.

Heading straight to her bedroom, she went to her walk-in closet and pulled down her TLC case and opened it up on the bed. She took out the listening devices, the recorder for the phone, and the mini digital camera. Just as a precaution she took out the two-ounce body lotion that had a separate compartment filled with a sedative — one never knew when it would come in handy. She looked at the pieces needed to assemble her gun. Hmm, not tonight, she thought.

She put the items in her black beaded purse. If anyone were to open it all they would see was a vain woman's array of makeup items. She smiled and closed the purse then put it on top of the dresser. Now for a quick shower then a tour through her closet.

"What time do you plan to get there tonight?" Steven asked Blake as they walked together to the employee garage.

"I figure around nine. She said it starts at eight, but I don't want her to have too much time to zero in on me."

"She's still giving you fever?" Steven chuckled.

"Worse."

Steven stopped short. "What do you mean?"

Blake shook his head slightly. "I can handle it." At least he hoped he could. He'd just be happy when this night was over, and prayed that Tristan would behave herself.

"Is there something that you're not telling me? Because if it affects this project I should know about it."

They approached Blake's silver Lexus first. He stopped and turned to his friend. "You have to swear not to say anything," he began.

Steven's smooth brown features crinkled. "What the hell is going on, man?"

Blake blew out a breath then slowly began to tell Steven what had occurred between him and Tristan and about her veiled threats.

Steven whistled through his teeth. "Damn. I don't even know what to say. Seems there should be somebody we can go to."

"But who? It would only make things worse, I'm sure. I'll figure it out."

"Do you think she would really pull the plug on the project if you don't sleep with her?"

"At this point I think Tristan Montgomery is capable of anything." He pressed the icon on his keychain and the car alarm deactivated, the locks opened and the powerful engine hummed to life. "See you tonight." He opened the door and slid onto the plush leather seat behind the wheel.

Steven leaned down by the driver's-side door. "My advice, my brother, keep Savannah glued to your hip. Your wife is no joke. If you can't keep the wolf away, Savannah can."

Blake had to chuckle. "I think you're right on that one." He shut the door. Steven stepped back as Blake rolled out of his parking space.

Steven waved and walked to his behemoth black Hummer several spaces away. Some guys have all the luck, he thought, or not.

When Blake arrived home, Savannah was just getting out of the shower. He tossed his keys on top of the dresser right next to Savannah's purse.

She stepped out of the master bath, wrapped in a towel just as Blake was coming out of his shirt.

When he saw her standing in the doorway, the light from the bathroom forming a halo around her and the steam from the shower wafting behind her, she truly was a vision. His heart banged in his chest and the soothing warmth of slinking down into a hot bath began to envelop him.

God, he loved this woman.

Her eyes brightened and she smiled. His insides ached.

"Hey," she said softly. "I didn't hear you come in."

"Hey, yourself." His voice was low and intimate. He crossed the room to where she stood and something came over him so powerful it was as if he'd lost all control and was guided only by desire.

"Blake?" Her eyes widened in question. But it was never answered. At least not in words.

Blake took her mouth in a searing kiss, no

build up, hot from the moment their lips met. He moaned deep in his belly, felt it rise up to his throat turning into a growl.

He snaked his fingers through her short pixie hair, pulled her head closer to his, sealing their lips. His tongue slid into her mouth, danced and dueled with hers as unadulterated lust raged through him. He backed her up against the wall, pinned her there with the weight of his muscled body and somehow managed to unbelt, unbutton and unzip his pants letting them pool at his feet. He kicked them away.

Blake's erection was so fiercely hard, so on fire that he knew if he didn't bury it deep inside her wetness soon he would combust. He pulled the towel away from her and tossed it to the floor next to his discarded pants.

His mouth left hers and snaked along her throat to the swell of her breasts that seemed to pulse of their own accord.

"Blake . . . baby . . ." she said, but still got no verbal response. Savannah's fingertips gripped his shoulders when his mouth encircled her right nipple and he teased it with the motion of his tongue. Her head lolled back, her legs trembled. He grabbed her full behind and lifted her off the floor. She wrapped her legs around his waist.

Their rapid breathing sounded like gushes of minigeysers filling the torrid air.

Savannah's slick, wet opening pressed against him. A light-headedness rushed through Blake when the sensitive tip of his penis found her.

He surged upward. Savannah cried out, a sound of exquisite delight to his ears. Blake pushed deep inside her and then remained motionless for a moment, relishing in the pure pleasure of their union. Then the muscles of her insides gripped him, sucked him in deeper and he lost his natural mind.

Suddenly Savannah was light as air when Blake began lifting her up and down on his erection as if she were no heavier than a loaf of bread. Stars exploded behind her eyes. The sensations were so intense that she forgot to breathe, to think.

Blake called out to God and everything holy as he loved up his wife with all that he had. Without breaking contact he walked with her to their bed, locked her beneath him, raised her legs above his shoulders then spread them as far as they would go.

"Look at me," he urged in a deep groan.

Savannah's eyes flicked open. Her heart stammered in her chest. She'd never seen that look of raw, almost savage hunger in his eyes before. It was as frightening as it was a sensual turn on.

Staring down into her sparkling eyes, Blake moved in and out of her, keeping her totally immobile as he took his pleasure.

They both began to tremble, murmur incomprehensible words of love as the power of what was happening between them became almost more than either of them could stand.

With a strength born out of desperate need, Savannah managed to raise her hips even higher, then down, back up again. She used the muscles inside her walls to jerk him.

Blake cried out to the heavens.

"Give it to me," she demanded. "All of you."

Blake got up on his knees, letting her legs stretch up toward his head.

"Like this?" he hissed as he pushed in and out of her, slow and hard.

Savannah whimpered. "More. More."

"How 'bout this?" He rotated his hips and he dove inside her again.

Her entire body began to shudder beginning at her toes, shimmying up her legs and thighs. Her breasts filled, her nipples stood on end. The world seemed to come to a grinding, crashing halt. The scream that erupted from her soul as her orgasm roared through her, vibrated in the air and raced through Blake's veins. He wound his hips again and again hitting that spot deep inside her over and over. His body suddenly went rigid as if he'd been shot with an electric charge as the uncontrolled grip and release of her wet walls sucked the life out of him. Every single drop.

Blake collapsed on top of her, his entire body trembling as he felt his penis continue to throb until he was sure he would go out of his mind with pleasure.

Savannah held him tightly against her, feeling the rapid-fire beating of their hearts, their hot breath beating in the air.

By degrees their pulses slowed and their heartbeats returned to a normal rhythm.

With much reluctance, Blake peeled himself away from Savannah and flipped over onto his back then turned on his side and drew Savannah close. "I love you," he whispered against her hair.

"I love you, too." She closed her eyes allowing the afterglow to flow through her.

"I think you may need another shower," he teased.

Savannah laughed lightly. "Yes, I think so. And you'll need one, too."

He spooned closer and cupped her breast

in his palm, its fullness overflowing over his fingers.

"Don't start," she warned. "Or we'll never get out of here."

"Maybe that's not such a bad idea," he offered, seeing a possible way out of what could be a touch-and-go evening.

Savannah's heart bumped. "Don't be silly. Although I'd love to spend the rest of the night with you, this is a great opportunity for you. You said so yourself." She hoped she sounded more encouraging than desperate. This was her best chance and she didn't want to blow getting inside Tristan Montgomery's house.

Blake heaved a sigh. "You're right," he conceded, kissing the back of her neck. "You wanna go first or should I?"

"You first." She flipped around to face him. Her gaze skimmed over his handsome face. "That was really special," she said softly.

His eyes crinkled in the corners when he smiled. "Only for you, baby."

Savannah pecked him on the lips. Whatever doubts she may have had lingering in her heart and mind were dispelled by the sincerity in his voice and in his eyes.

"Go get ready," she said.

Blake kissed her one last time and got up

from the bed.

Savannah lay back against the thick damp pillows. She folded her hands across her stomach and looked up at the ceiling then around the room at the turbulence they'd caused. Since the beginning of their relationship, she and Blake had always had traffic-stopping lovemaking sessions. But this one was for the record books. She still tingled from deep inside. How she was going to manage to concentrate on being social tonight while handling her business and not think about getting her husband back between the sheets was a mystery to her.

But, multitasking was her middle name, she thought, sitting up. But first things first, find that drop-dead outfit.

CHAPTER 13

Blake held Savannah's hand as she descended the steps of their town house. She glanced up to see a black Lincoln Town Car equipped with a driver waiting for them at the curb. She turned to Blake. Her brows rose in question.

"I forgot to mention that Tristan sent a car for us. It's at our disposal for the night."

"Oh," was all she could mutter. This Tristan was pulling out all the stops, she thought. If this was the prelude for the evening, they were in store for a treat. She took her husband's arm.

"My name is William," the driver said with a slight bow of his head. He opened the door and helped Savannah inside. "Ms. Montgomery has a full set up for you in the car. Please enjoy."

Blake got in beside his wife and William shut the door behind them. They both looked at each other and giggled. The luxurious interior came complete with piped in music, a phone, internet access, full bar, chilled appetizers of cocktail shrimp, smoked salmon, pâté and an assortment of crackers and dips, a sunroof and a sound-proof partition in case they wanted some privacy.

"Does she treat all of her architects this way?" Savannah asked, testing out the GPA system.

"Got me." Blake reached for a shrimp.

Savannah opened her mouth to allow Blake to pop a shrimp into it. She chewed thoughtfully. Maybe she was simply being paranoid considering what she planned to do when she arrived at Chez Montgomery, she thought cattily. But that unsettled feeling was creeping up again. Each time she put her husband and Tristan Montgomery's name together her stomach would do a nosedive. She wanted to chalk it up to the job at hand but her women's intuition and a wife's instincts had her feeling much differently.

"Is Steven coming?" Savannah finally asked to take her mind off her disturbing thoughts.

"Yes, he said he was coming. I'm curious to see who he will have on his arm this time. I can't remember ever going out with Steven and seeing the same woman twice." He chuckled and went for another shrimp.

"Do you ever wish you were single?" she asked out of the blue.

Blake choked, coughing until water began to run out of his eyes. Savannah banged his back with one hand, grabbed a bottle of water with the other, stuck the bottle between her knees and twisted the top off.

"Here, drink this." She tilted the bottle to his head. He took a gurgling swallow, coughed some more.

Blake drew in a long lungful of much needed air, sputtering a lingering cough and took another swig of water. "Whew! Thought I was a goner there for a minute."

Savannah took one of the linen napkins from the tray and dribbled it with water then patted his face. "Feeling better?"

"Yeah, much," he said. He shook his head. "Shrimp must have gone down the wrong way."

Savannah looked at him askance. "Probably so. Told you about wolfing down food." She put on a smile.

"I was starving, especially after earlier this evening. You drained me." He leaned over and kissed her forehead. "Thanks for saving me from myself." He chuckled.

"Anytime."

Blake adjusted his tie, wiped his face with the damp napkin then relaxed against the smooth leather. "This is the life, isn't it baby? Just think, another job like this development and we can live exactly like this — chauffeurs, penthouses, beach houses, brand-new cars right off the lot and enough money for a thunderstorm, forget a rainy day." He chuckled then draped his arm around her shoulder and pulled her closer. "I want to do that for you," he said, his voice sounding urgent. "I want you to have everything, and whatever it takes I'm going to make sure that you do."

Alarms jangled in her head. She turned in his arm to look in his eyes. "Blake, I don't need all of the trappings. I would be happy with you in a hut — with lights and gas, of course — but I don't want all of this. All I want is you and a family. That's it."

He ran a finger slowly across her bottom lip until she trembled. "That's why I love you. And that's why I'm going to make sure that you have the life that you deserve."

She stared at him for a moment before turning away, knowing that there was no point in debating or arguing the point, at least not now. She gazed out the window. Yellow cabs darted in and out of traffic, horns blared and the distant wail of an ambulance siren could be heard in the distance. Pedestrians from the barely dressed to Broadway fabulous combed the streets. All one incredible sight to behold yet none of it was connected, each element was all part of the landscape but totally unrelated to each other. In between it all, the bright lights of the Manhattan skyscrapers, all-night eateries and nightclubs flashed like warning beacons. When had they fallen off the same page? When had they stopped wanting the same things?

The limo crossed Fifth Avenue and the visual ambiance was almost immediate. Gone were the throngs of people, noise and businesses entreating customers. This was the East side of Manhattan. And as the limo glided along Park Avenue the life of the rich and famous became plainly obvious. This was old money, original New York money earned from bootlegging, shipping, oil and cars. This was the land of Rockefellers, Fords, Astors, Huttons, Hiltons and Trumps — the upper stratosphere of wealth, a land where a luxury apartment could easily run eight to ten thousand dollars per month. Where nannies abounded, and purebred puppies had playdates.

The intercom chirped. Blake leaned forward and pressed a white button.

"We'll be arriving in approximately three minutes," William informed them.

Savannah and Blake turned to each other and stifled giggles.

Savannah cleared her throat. "Thank you, William." She covered her mouth to hold back her laughter.

In precisely three minutes the limo rolled to a stop in front of Tristan Montgomery's posh Sutton Place digs. The stately three-story town house looked like every other one of its ilk within the quiet enclave. But, as Savannah knew firsthand, looks were deceiving.

William came around and opened the door, helping Savannah alight from the car.

"I'll be at your disposal for the evening." He handed them a miniature walkie-talkie. "Call whenever you are ready." He tipped his head and returned to his seat.

Savannah slipped her hand through the crook in Blake's arm and walked toward the entrance. Muted sounds could be heard coming from the other side of the door. Blake rang a bell that neither of them could hear. Moments later, like something right out of a Joan Crawford movie, a tuxedoed butler opened the door.

"Welcome and good evening. Your names, please?"

"Blake and Savannah Fields," Blake offered.

A tight smile tugged his mouth. "Please, come in. The guests are in the sitting room."

The gentle sounds of something soothing played in the rarified air. Chandeliers that sparkled like diamonds hung from the cathedral ceiling. To the right, a wall to wall window looked out upon The East River.

Savannah's heels clicked against the white marble floor in concert to the ping of champagne glasses and tinkling laughter coming from in front of them.

They were led a short distance and before them the sitting room, which was as big as their entire home, opened before them. Diamonds, platinum, emeralds and white gold blinged and popped like paparazzi blubs.

There were about forty guests milling about the lush space. A dozen or more waist-high tubular tables were set up around the room, draped in white linen, some surrounded by guests nibbling on hors d'oeuvres generously being distributed by more waiters and waitresses than a five-star restaurant.

"Is that 'the Donald'?" Savannah whispered behind her hand.

"Yeah, I think so. And that's the guy from

134

60 Minutes."

There were other familiar faces from newspapers, television and film, huddling in comfortable lounge chairs or milling about at the bar or tables.

At least she was dressed for the part, Savannah thought. Her Chanel cocktail dress was a perfect fit for this high-heeled crowd.

"Blake! There you are."

They turned to the voice behind them.

Stunning was the first word that entered Savannah's mind when she laid eyes on Tristan Montgomery. She was taller than Savannah had imagined — at least five foot ten, curvy yet slender at the same time, a goddess's body. Everything around her seemed to flow — from her catwalk to her shoulder-length hair to the nearly sheer, wide-legged white evening pants that she wore. Her skin was flawless, the color of warm honey. But it was her eyes that were most arresting, perfectly shaped almonds with thick lashes that shadowed the secrets beneath. Her mouth was full with what men would call "kissable lips." Diamonds hung from her tiny lobes, embraced her right wrist and dotted her long neck.

"Did my driver pick you up on time?"

"Yes, and thanks again."

She tossed back her head, revealing the long lines of her throat. "Don't be silly. How many times do I have to remind you how special you are? And special people deserve special treatment." She said all of this with her hand trailing up and down Blake's arm.

Then as if she'd been given her cue, she seemed to notice Savannah for the first time. She turned a discerning eye on the wife of the man she coveted. She put on her best smile, flashing milky white, perfectly straight teeth.

"I am so rude. You must be Sarah." She extended her hand.

"This is my wife, *Savannah,*" Blake quickly corrected. "Sweetheart, this is Tristan Montgomery."

Tristan's free hand flew to her ample bosom in mock embarrassment. "Oh, please excuse me Savannah, I am so horrible with names. I'm sure Blake could verify that." She laughed. "I can't remember one of my assistant's names from the other. Welcome to my little gathering. Please make yourself comfortable. Dinner will be served in about twenty minutes. I'm only waiting on the Secretary General." She shook her head sadly. "He only lives right down the street and he's never on time. Oh, please excuse me for just a moment. I must say hello to the congressman. Blake, why don't you come with me? I want to introduce you." She snatched him away before either he or Savannah could blink.

Tristan floated away with her husband, leaving her distinctive scent behind. The same scent she'd smelled on her husband's clothing.

Her stomach knotted and ugly images formed in her head. The room seemed to disappear and she was standing in its center alone, confused and angry. She looked across the room and Tristan was holding on to Blake as if he was *her* man. They looked like a couple.

Suddenly she felt ill. She turned. Her stomach lurched to her throat.

"Are you all right, miss?" a tiny waitress asked.

"Ladies' room," was all she could get out.

"Right down the hall on your left."

As she darted out of the room with as much composure as she could summon, she silently prayed that she wouldn't make a spectacle of herself before she reached the bathroom. *And, Lord, please don't let there be a line.*

Mercifully, the bathroom was empty. She rushed in and locked the door and immediately turned on the cold water full blast. She took handfuls, cupping the water to her mouth then patted her head.

Drawing in ragged breaths, she slowly lifted her head and looked in the mirror.

Truth looked right back at her.

Blake was having an affair with Tristan Montgomery. The nausea was slowly becoming replaced with a pain that was inexplicable. Could hearts actually break?

Her eyes burned with tears of anguish and fury. How long had it been going on? Did he come here? Terrible, dark thoughts raced through her mind.

She needed to confront him. Plain and simple. Ask him outright if he was sleeping with another woman. What if he said yes? What in heaven's name would she do? Did he love her? Would he leave her for Tristan?

Oh, God! She leaned over the sink, drawing in long, deep breaths, trying to slow her racing heart and the pounding in her temples.

She knew if she asked Blake, he would deny it. He would deny it as easily as he'd denied the perfume on his shirt.

Savannah glanced at her purse sitting on the edge of the sink. Everything she needed to discover the truth was right inside. She opened her purse and took out the compact that held the listening devices. She held it up in her hand. Her expression became resolute. She was here to do a job for TLC, uncover the truth behind Montgomery Enterprises. As she stepped out of the bathroom, scanning the spaces for the perfect hiding places, she wondered if what she was about to do was for the good of the assignment or her marriage.

CHAPTER 14

The rest of the night was a blur to Savannah. All of her concentration was focused on setting the devices and not strangling her husband and his lover. She vaguely heard Tristan as she went on and on about the legacy of Sutton Place and all the who's who that had resided there over the years.

"They recently finished filming a movie with that gorgeous Denzel Washington. I tried to get him to come tonight but he's on the coast," Tristan was saying. "This would be of interest to you, Blake," she trilled on, "the famous architect I.M. Pei lived here, as well. Isn't that wonderful. Not to mention that Marilyn Monroe and her then husband, Arthur Miller, were former residents."

Savannah nodded and smiled. She'd managed to "accidentally" stumble into Tristan's bedroom and plant a device above a Picasso painting before the maid found her. There was one near the front door, tucked beneath the table and another right here in the "sitting room."

"With the kind of money and notoriety that Blake is going to receive from this redevelopment job, you two may want to think about getting a place here, as well." She smiled at Blake.

Said the spider to the fly, Savannah thought.

"We're happy where we are on Sugar Hill," Savannah said, without gritting her teeth. "The house has been in the family for decades."

Blake put his arm around Savannah's waist and drew her close. "Yes, we have a beautiful home that we love very much. Something to pass down to our kids one day." He looked down lovingly at Savannah and she wondered if he was vying for best actor or if he really meant it.

"Don't mean to interrupt, folks," Steven said, joining the trio, "but Karen and I are going to be heading home." He turned to Tristan and stretched out his hand, which she took. "Great party. Thanks for having us."

"Yes, thank you," his date, Karen said.

Steven turned to Blake and patted his back. "See you in the office on Monday." He leaned over and kissed Savannah's cheek. "Great to see you as always." He leaned close to her ear and whispered, "Don't let her rattle you." He stepped back, took his date by the hand. " 'Night, everyone." He waved and walked out.

"We probably need to be going, as well," Blake said.

"Oh, no. So early? The night is still young."

Blake chuckled. "Savannah and I have plans for tomorrow."

Tristan turned to Savannah. "If you want to go home early and get some rest, I can get William to drive you. There are still a few people I want Blake to meet." She took Blake's arm as if she were actually going to snatch him away.

"I don't think so," Savannah said. "One thing my mother always taught me, you come in with a man, you leave with him." Her hard gaze locked with Tristan's.

For a tense moment, nothing was said. Tristan laughed. "You have a wise mother." She blew out a breath. "Well, if you must leave, I'll stop by the office on Monday. There are a few things I want to go over with you."

"Fine. Thanks for a great evening."

"Pleasure to meet you, Savannah. You have a wonderful husband, but I'm sure you know that."

Savannah took Blake's hand. "Yes, I do. Good night and enjoy the rest of your evening."

By the time they reached the front door, Savannah was shaking all over. Anger replaced the blood in her veins and it raced through her like a tidal wave.

"Enjoy yourself?" Blake asked once they were settled inside the limo.

"Great time," she bit out.

Blake turned to her with a frown on his face. "Are you all right? You're as stiff as a board."

"I feel a headache coming on, that's all. Must have been the wine." She turned her head to look out the window to keep from looking at him.

Blake pressed back into the seat. "Are you sure that's it — a headache?"

"That's what I said, didn't I? Why would I lie to you?" Her throat knotted.

Blake threw up his hands in surrender. "Okay, okay. Sorry I asked."

They both moved to their respective corners of the car — and later that night in bed, as well.

When Savannah awoke the following morning, she found Blake's side of the bed empty. She turned onto her back and stared up at the ceiling. Last night was the first time in their six years of marriage that she had not fallen asleep in her husband's arms. Her heart lurched in her chest as the previous evening ran through her head in full color.

Savannah still could not believe that Tristan would be so bold and brazen as to drape herself all over Blake as if she didn't even exist. What was worse was that Blake didn't seem to mind. Her jaw tightened. She guessed he wouldn't.

Footsteps approaching the bedroom door drew her attention. She glanced toward it.

"Good morning, sleepyhead. You were resting so peacefully I didn't want to disturb you." He approached the bed and sat down next to her.

"Feeling better this morning? How's your headache."

She pushed herself up into a sitting position and drew the sheet up to her chin then realized she had nothing to cover up as she'd slept with a nightgown on, something she hadn't done since the first night of their honeymoon. She wondered if Blake even noticed — or cared.

"Good morning," she murmured. "Headache's fine."

"Great. I promised Gwynne we would be there around one."

Blake's younger sister, Gwynne, had recently given birth to a beautiful baby girl a bit more than a month ago. Blake hadn't seen his niece since she was brought home from the hospital and had been promising Gwynne that he'd come out and see them both.

As much as she loved Gwynne and her husband, Alex, seeing a loving family with a brand-new baby was something she just couldn't handle today.

"For some reason I'm really tired," she said, unable to meet his eyes. "I know I'm not up to a car ride all the way to Philadelphia today. Please give my love to Gwynne and Alex and kisses for Mikayla."

She got out of bed and headed for the bathroom. Blake grabbed her by the shoulder and turned her around.

"You want to tell me what the hell is going on with you? You've been treating me like I've got something you can catch ever since last night. You think I didn't notice the granny gown you went to bed in? What's up? Talk to me."

She looked into his eyes and saw the hurt and concern hovering there waiting for answers.

It was on her lips but she could not say the words or ask the question. The fear of his answer was greater than her desire to know.

"Nothing. Just out of sorts, that's all." She gently touched his arm and sparks, as always, ran through her. "I'm sorry." She went into the bathroom, shutting the door behind her.

When she emerged a half hour later, bathed and wrapped in her favorite sky-blue terry cloth robe, Blake was standing at the dresser putting his wallet in the front pocket of his jeans. He turned toward her.

"I'm going to head out," he said almost to himself. "I should be back before it gets too late. If I decide to stay over I'll give you a call." He didn't wait for her response. He walked out and moments later she heard the front door shut.

That's when the tears came, silent, burning and painful. She curled up on the bed and wept.

CHAPTER 15

Dani and Nia pulled up in front of Savannah's house. Danielle put the SUV in Park.

"You really think we should do this?" Nia asked, suddenly not so sure of their bright idea.

"Look, Savannah is our girl. If Blake is messing around on her, she deserves to know. Wouldn't you want to know?"

Nia's brows bunched together for a minute. "Yeah, I guess. But this kind of thing always turns out badly. I don't want this to ruin our friendship. You know the old saying about shooting the messenger."

Dani cut her gaze in Nia's direction then rolled her eyes. "Let's go. I'd rather she be pissed off at us than to see her on the eleven o'clock news with a jacket over her face while reporters ask her why she ran over her husband a dozen times in the parking lot."

Nia grimaced at the image. "You're probably right."

They got out and marched up the steps to the front door. Dani rang the bell.

"Maybe she's not home," Nia said after several moments.

Dani glanced down the street and pointed. "There's her car over there."

Nia followed Dani's outstretched finger. "I don't see Blake's Lexus. Maybe they're together."

Dani rang the bell again, pressing hard and long.

From the other side of the door they heard a faint voice ask who was there.

Dani and Nia looked at each other, concern etched on their faces.

"Savannah, it's me and Nia. Open up, girl. Got us standing out here like vacuum salespeople."

"Don't feel like company."

Dani knocked on the door. "Savannah. Open the door! You're scaring me. You know I'll call the damned po po if you don't."

Several moments passed before they heard the locks disengaged. The door slowly opened. Savannah stepped aside and let her girlfriends in.

"Why is it so damned dark in here?" Dani demanded to know.

"Look you wanted to come in so now

you're in. Don't start bitching." Savannah stormed off toward the kitchen.

Dani's brows rose to her hairline.

"Maybe we should have left her alone," Nia whispered.

"Aw, hell, naw. Something is up and she's gonna tell me before I leave outta here today. And put your damned glasses on. Can't you see she's a mess?" She followed Savannah into the kitchen, pulled out a chair from beneath the table and sat down.

Savannah had her face buried in the interior of the refrigerator.

"You're gonna talk to us, Anna. We're your girls. Whatever it is . . ."

Nia slowly took a seat, as well. "Three heads and shoulders are better than one, honey."

Savannah wiped her face with the sleeve of her robe. She drew in a shuddering breath. She knew she couldn't stay in the fridge for the rest of the afternoon and she also knew that Dani was the most stubborn person on the planet. She would sit there until doomsday.

Slowly she turned around.

Both Nia and Dani's mouths opened in silent exclamations of shock. Savannah might never grace the cover of *Essence* or *Glamour* magazine for looks, but she was still a good-looking woman. This Savannah Fields, however, neither of them recognized. The whites of her eyes were red and her lids were so swollen she looked as if she'd done twelve rounds with the champ.

Dani rose from her seat. "What the hell is going on?" She rushed around the table to where Savannah stood. She lifted Savannah's chin to force her to focus. "Did he hit you? 'Cause, I swear, if he . . ."

Savannah shook her head back and forth. "No. No, nothing like that." She drew in a breath. "I wish he would have. It would have been less painful." She moved away from Dani and went to sit down at the table.

Seeing the pain and anguish on her friend's face, forced Nia to shake away any reservations she may have had about getting all up in Savannah's business.

"You need to tell us what's going on. Right now," Nia said. "Where's Blake?"

"He went out. To his sister's house in Philly."

"Have you eaten anything?" Nia asked.

"Not hungry."

"Well, I am. I'm going to fix us something and then we are going to talk."

Dani went to the side counter and turned on the radio. Then she opened the kitchen window and the blinds. Soft music and the warmth of the afternoon sun floated into the room. Within moments the atmosphere softened and the tenseness in Savannah's chest began to ease.

Nia was whipping out pots, defrosting meat in the microwave and chopping up green onions and tomatoes. She found several packs of shredded cheeses in the vegetable bin and took those out along with a package of soft taco shells.

Before long the kitchen was filled with the mouthwatering aroma of grilling ground beef sautéed in spices.

Dani got out dishes and glasses and set the table. "How about some wine?" she asked.

Savannah nodded. Dani headed off to the living room and checked the liquor cabinet. She found a bottle of red wine, filled the ice bucket with ice and stuck the bottle in the ice to chill.

Nia finished up with the beans and rice then shredded some lettuce and mashed three avocados. She took a large platter from the cabinet and put it on the counter. She gently warmed the taco shells then placed them on the tray. In one mixing bowl she added the beans and rice, in another was her special guacamole dip, then the shredded cheeses, lettuce and tomatoes.

151

She balanced the tray and set it down on the center of the table. In less than thirty minutes she'd created a small feast.

"Black bean soup would have been perfect, but it needs time to simmer," Nia murmured.

Nia was certainly the cook in the trio. She could make something out of nothing even without her glasses. She'd confessed to them once that her childhood dream was to be a chef. The closest she'd come, however, was being an advocate for all the restaurants and cafes in the city.

"Well, eat up," she said, reaching for a taco and quickly beginning to fill it to overflowing.

The ladies dug in, then began filling their glasses with the rich red wine. Before long, Savannah actually began to smile as she listened to Dani talk about her latest "sexcapade" with a model.

"Dani, you are crazy," Nia said, with a chuckle. "That man ain't even a man, he's still a boy. What twenty-five?"

"But," Nia said, holding up a finger for emphasis. "What he lacks in experience he makes up for in enthusiasm."

The trio cracked up laughing.

"And where did you meet this underage Adonis?" Savannah asked, uttering her first words since she agreed to the wine.

"I was doing a photo shoot at the Pause for Men day spa on 135th Street for a *Men's Health* magazine spread. They're doing an article on workout attire for men. He was one of the guys at the spa. We exchanged numbers and the rest was . . . incredible." A wicked grin stretched across her generous mouth.

Nia shook her head and chuckled then turned to Savannah. "Speaking of men. We've politely danced around you for a couple of hours now, Anna. You can't tell us there's nothing wrong."

Savannah stared into two pairs of concerned eyes. If nothing else she knew she had the support and love of her girlfriends. They may get on each other's nerves from time to time but when the dust settled it was the three of them against the world. She reached for her glass of wine and held it out to Nia for a refill then took a long swallow. She put the glass down but kept her hand wrapped around it as if it was some secret source of strength.

With great effort she spilled out the story about Blake and Tristan. Everything she felt and all that she saw. She did, however, leave out the tiny little detail about her working for TLC.

Nia and Dani looked at each other once Savannah was done. Nia gave an imperceptible shake of her head, no.

"What can we do to help?" Dani asked taking her cue from Nia.

Savannah lowered her head. "I wish I knew. Right now I'm still trying to process it all."

"What if you're wrong?" Nia asked, even as she doubted her own question.

"You need to talk to Blake. Put your feelings on the table."

"And what if he lies to me? What then?" Her gaze pleaded for an answer that she could handle.

"It could all be nothing. Blake is one fine brother. Any woman in her right mind would be attracted to him — including Tristan Montgomery," Dani said.

"Exactly. And it doesn't mean he feels the same way about her." Nia leaned forward and took Savannah's hand. "Blake loves the ground you walk on."

A glimmer of a smile tugged at Savannah's mouth.

"How do you feel about Blake?" Nia gently asked.

The knot grew in Savannah's throat. "He's my . . . soul, my life. I can't imagine going through my days without him." Tears shimmered in her eyes.

"Then fight for your husband and your marriage," Dani said, slapping her palm on the table. "Don't you dare roll over and play dead."

"That's *your* man and Tristan Montgomery needs to know that."

They were right, Savannah realized, looking from one determined face to the other, and she knew exactly what she was going to do next.

CHAPTER 16

How she got through the rest of the weekend while playing the contrite, dutiful wife,
was a minor miracle in Savannah's mind.
She was visibly relieved when she opened
her eyes on Monday morning and prepared
for work.

By the time Blake had returned Saturday
evening from visiting with his sister, she'd
fixed a dinner fit for a king. Scented candles
flickered throughout the house, soft music
played in the background and she greeted
him in a black lace thong and nothing else.

As she made wild, uninhibited love to her
husband, in the back of her mind she
thought that at the very least she'd wear
him out so bad he wouldn't have the energy
for anyone else. Sunday, as usual, had been
a breeze as Blake assumed his position on
the couch.

"Good morning, Richard," Savannah
chimed as she walked into the office kitchen.

"Hi. You're mighty chipper this morning. Have a good weekend?" He poured a cup of coffee and added enough sugar to go into shock.

Savannah watched and grimaced. "Can't complain. And you?" She went to the fridge in search of some OJ.

"Went sailing with the family out on Sag Harbor."

Richard was a frustrated sailor trapped in a lawyer's body. Every chance he got, he was on the water in his boat.

Savannah poured a tall glass of juice. "Well, I'd better get busy. I have those briefs of yours to prepare."

Richard checked his watch. "I have a discovery hearing to attend at ten. Hopefully it won't take too long. We can go over the brief when I get back."

"I'll be ready." She took her glass and headed to her desk. Besides preparing a brief she had other things on her agenda.

Savannah worked feverishly for two hours. Finally the brief was completed, checked and rechecked. She printed out all of the supporting documents and put everything in a folder just as Richard returned from court. She held up the folder with a triumphant grin.

Richard took the folder. "Gotta hand it to

you, Savannah, you are the best. I'll take a look and we can review, in say, about a half hour."

Savannah stole a quick glance at the overhead clock. Eleven. "Sure."

He tapped the folder against the desk then walked away to his office. The instant he was out of earshot, Savannah picked up the phone and dialed. Her heart hammered in her chest.

The phone rang twice before it was picked up. "Montgomery Enterprises."

"Good morning. I was hoping to speak to Ms. Montgomery."

"I'm sorry, Ms. Montgomery is busy. I'll be happy to take a message."

"I'm sure she'll want to speak to me. I'm Mrs. Fields, wife of Blake Fields, the architect on the Brooklyn project."

"Please hold. I'll see if Ms. Montgomery can be disturbed."

Savannah tugged on her bottom lip with her teeth as she waited for what seemed an eternity.

"Sarah!" Tristan's voice trilled through the line.

"Savannah. Hello, Ms. Montgomery."

"Oh, please excuse me. Why can't I remember names? What can I do for you?"

"I wanted to personally call you and tell

you what a wonderful time I had at your gathering on Friday."

"That wasn't necessary. But thank you for calling."

"You have such a beautiful home." Savannah nervously tapped her foot. "And I felt like royalty the entire night. I simply never knew what famous face was going to show up next. You seem to know everyone who's anyone." Savannah laughed lightly.

"I do have wonderful friends."

Savannah could hear the smile in her voice and the slow shift in her formal tone.

"I'm happy that you enjoyed yourself enough to make a personal call. Not many people do that."

"I have to blame it on my upbringing."

"Well, if there's nothing else. I have a full day ahead of me. As a matter of fact, I'm supposed to see your husband later."

"Actually I wanted to ask you . . . um, what is the name of that fabulous perfume you were wearing?"

"Oh . . . Do you like it?"

"Love it. It's so . . . unique."

"To be truthful, I have it specially prepared."

"You're kidding." Her foot tapped faster.

"If you really like it, I'd be happy to give you the information to the guy I use."

"Would you? Oh, you are truly a jewel. I was wondering, Blake has said such fabulous things about you and your business, I was wondering . . . I mean, I know it may be an imposition, but I was hoping I could stop by your office and look around. He can't stop talking about the decor and I've really been thinking about redecorating our town house. And your taste is impeccable." She held her breath, knew how utterly stupid it sounded but she was relying on Tristan's vanity.

"Well, since you put it that way. Sure, why not? How about next week?"

"I was thinking this afternoon. Say lunchtime? One-thirty? I was going to be in your area."

Tristan blew out a breath. "I . . . suppose that would be fine. I can't spend much time. As I said I have an appointment today."

"I totally understand. I would simply love to get some ideas and . . . surprise Blake."

"Fine. Come by."

Zero for common sense and point one for vanity. "Thank you so much. I'll see you soon."

When she hung up the phone her hands were shaking. She checked the clock. She had a little more than an hour to get it together. She grabbed her purse and darted into Richard's office.

"Richard, sorry for busting in, but something has come up. I need to run out and I may not be back."

He swept his reading glasses from the bridge of his nose and looked across at her from his seated position behind his desk.

"Is everything all right? Something I can do?"

Savannah held up her hand. "No, I'm fine. Just something I need to take care of right away and it may take longer than a couple of hours, that's all. I'll be here first thing in the morning and we can go over the brief then if you have any questions."

"Sure . . . okay," he answered slowly. "See you tomorrow."

"Thanks." She spun away and rushed out. By the time she got to her car it was nearly noon. If she could beat traffic she could do what she needed to do and get to Ms. Tristan's in time.

Her first stop was Neiman Marcus on Fifth Avenue. She went straight to the designer floor. She knew exactly what she was looking for. She'd seen the dress in a catalog and fell in love with it. It was totally out of her price range but she didn't care.

After about twenty minutes, she found the dress, paid for it and quickly changed in the dressing room along with her new shoes and matching purse. The last thing to do was to transfer her surveillance devices from her old purse to her new one. She took one last look in the triple mirror.

When she emerged, she was the African-American version of Audrey Hepburn from *Breakfast at Tiffany's.* Her discarded clothing was tucked away in her Neiman Marcus bag. She checked her watch — twelve forty-five. She headed for the makeup counter, for a complete free makeover with the purchase of select products, of course.

At one-ten Savannah was strolling out, redone from head to toe. She had twenty minutes to get across town to Montgomery Enterprises.

Savannah pulled up in front of Trump Tower, where Montgomery Enterprises was housed. A valet met her car at the curb.

"How long will you be, ma'am?"

Savannah grabbed her purse, left her keys in the ignition and stepped out. "No more than an hour." She glanced upward at the towering building of glass and steel then walked through the revolving doors.

Montgomery Enterprises was located on the fortieth floor. She stepped off the elevator into what could be considered no less than a spectacular reception area. White dominated the space, punctuated by glass tables, crystal cut bowls, strategically placed mirrors, a horseshoe-shaped glass reception desk and bursts of color from exotic tropical blooms set in tubular glass vases. She felt as if she should take off her shoes as her heels sank into the plush white carpet.

Savannah proceeded to the front desk.

"Good afternoon. Welcome to ME. How may I help you?"

"I'm here to see Ms. Montgomery. My name is Savannah Fields."

"Yes, Ms. Montgomery is expecting you. Why don't you have a seat for a moment?"

Savannah gave a short nod and turned to take a seat on the long, sleek white leather sofa.

Moments later a young woman who looked like she should be on the cover of Vogue approached Savannah.

"Mrs. Fields?"

Savannah looked up from perusing a magazine. "Yes . . ."

"Ms. Montgomery will see you now. If you will follow me."

Savannah's heart thumped in her chest. She put on her best smile, picked up her purse and followed the ingenue down the wide corridor.

Each of the offices she passed had glass fronts. It was almost eerie in that she felt that each of the employees was on some sort of display and that privacy was not an option at Montgomery Enterprises.

The stopped at the first office that was not glass enclosed. Instead it had a thick, maple door with embossed gold. The young woman knocked lightly and turned the knob.

The door opened onto what was no less than paradise. Whereas all of what she'd seen so far had given a sleek almost sterile illusion, Tristan's space burst with color; from tropical fish in an enormous tank that covered one wall to the muted lighting and deep burgundy carpeting. Tristan was seated behind a huge desk that matched the door. Flowers bloomed on tabletops and covered the sill from end to end. This was certainly not what Savannah expected. A portrait of Tristan and a man Savannah assumed was her father graced one wall. A forty-two-inch television took up another. Leather furnishings matched the rich-colored carpet to perfection.

Tristan acknowledged Savannah's presence with a raised index finger as she finished up her phone conversation. She placed the phone on the cradle.

"Mrs. Fields. Sorry for the wait. I was tying up some loose ends and I'm sure you know how those can be." Her smile missed her eyes. She stood. "Please have a seat." She came from behind her desk and sat opposite Savannah in an armchair. "So, what do you think so far about what you've seen?" she asked, getting straight to the business at hand.

"Stunning. This office space is incredible," she said with sincerity.

"Would you believe I did it all myself?"

Savannah's brows rose in surprise. "Really?"

Tristan's smile was filled with pride. "Actually I attended Fashion Institute of Technology right here in New York. My major was interior design. My father, of course, thought it just a frivolous activity and demanded that I take business courses, as well. When he died, I redid the entire office to suit me." She chuckled. "He's probably spinning in his grave as we speak."

She folded her hands on top of her desk. A diamond flashed on her right hand. "So, I can have someone show you around. I'm not really sure how office decor would fit with a town house." She gazed at her curiously.

"After being in your home, I had to see

what your work space looked like. I thought that I'd somehow be able to take ideas from both." That sounded pretty good. "And as I said, Blake can't stop raving about it. Maybe I can even make some suggestions to my boss about updating our offices." She smiled.

Tristan gave a slight shrug of her left shoulder. "I have a meeting in about five minutes. I'll have one of the assistants show you around."

"That would be perfect. I can't thank you enough."

Tristan stood, gathered some folders from her desk and locked her drawer. "You can wait here. Someone will be in shortly. Make yourself comfortable." She came from behind her desk. Savannah stood up and extended her hand.

"I really appreciate this."

Tristan shook her hand, looked her hard in the eye. "Anything for Blake."

Savannah's heart stood still for an instant then raced. Tristan turned and walked out.

Savannah stood rock still. It wasn't so much what Tristan said, it was *how* she said it and the look of blatant predatory gleam in her eyes. Savannah drew in a breath.

"An eye for an eye" as the Good Book says. And hell hath no fury like a woman fighting to save her marriage. She glanced quickly around, her mission clear. She took what she needed from her purse and moved expertly around the office. Everything she'd ever learned about surveillance rushed to the forefront of her thoughts, fighting for space against the images of Blake and Tristan. She worked with a single-minded purpose — get Tristan Montgomery and save her marriage.

By the time the young woman who'd escorted her to Tristan's office came to take her on the tour, Savannah had successfully planted two listening devices in Tristan's office and had taken a seat. One was hidden in a plant directly behind her desk, the other tucked beneath the center conference table. She'd also installed a mini video camera that was no bigger than a penny — and nearly as flat as a piece of paper — right on the frame of the portrait of Tristan and her father. The black dot blended perfectly with the frame.

"If you're ready, I'll be happy to show you around," the woman said with the same smile as before.

"Thank you." Savannah rose. "You have no idea how much I appreciate this."

"No problem." The woman headed for the door.

"Oh, one second. I'm sorry." Savannah pulled out her BlackBerry, which had been specially configured. Feigning checking for messages, she located the right code, pressed Send and activated the devices hidden in the office. Now she would be able to access any activity from her BlackBerry and from her laptop.

She popped her BlackBerry into her purse, and beamed a smile. "Ready!"

CHAPTER 17

Blake wasn't looking forward to his meeting with Tristan. Since their last private encounter he'd been successful at keeping her at bay. Knowing Tristan, however, he knew it wouldn't last long. At some point he knew there would be a showdown.

His intercom buzzed. "Yes?"

"Ms. Montgomery is here."

"Show her to the conference room. Thanks."

He drew in a long breath of resolve. This was business. He intended to keep it that way. He grabbed his jacket from the back of his chair and slipped it on then headed for the conference room. Steven stopped him in the hallway.

"Hey, man, I was on my way to your office."

"Why? We have a meeting with Tristan."

"Yeah, I know. That's why I was coming to see you. I just got a call from my brother's wife, Monica. Carl was in a pretty bad car accident. I need to get to the hospital."

Blake grabbed Steven's shoulder and squeezed. "Man, I'm sorry. Did she say how he was?"

"Monica was so hysterical I barely made out where they'd taken him. Finally figured out she was saying South Orange General in New Jersey."

Blake eyed his friend. Steven was the coolest guy he knew, nothing rattled him. But he could see how badly shaken he was. Carl was Steven's baby brother and they were really close.

"Listen, go. Call me the minute you hear something and if there's anything I can do you let me know."

Steven nodded numbly. "Thanks. Listen, I wish I could be there in that meeting . . ."

"Don't worry about me. I can handle it. Go."

Steven gave a short nod and jogged to the elevator. Blake uttered a silent prayer that Carl would be just fine then headed off to meet the next disaster waiting to happen.

Blake continued down the corridor then turned right at the fork in the hallway and walked down to the conference room. He opened the door ready to do battle but found the room empty. He stepped all the way in and looked around. Not a sign of Tristan. She'd been there. Her scent was still in the air.

He walked to the phone and dialed from the desk. "Jasmine, where is Ms. Montgomery?"

"In the conference room."

"No, she's not."

"Maybe she went to the restroom."

"Did she come alone?"

"Yes, sir."

"Thank you, Jasmine." He hung up the phone. He was getting a bad feeling.

Fifteen minutes passed and no Tristan. Finally he left and returned to his office, the whole incident pissing him off more than making him curious.

He threw open the door of his office and there was Tristan sitting behind his desk with her feet propped up.

"I thought you'd never get here."

He kept the door open. "We had a meeting in the conference room." He stepped farther into the room.

She brought her legs to the floor and spun the chair away from the desk and stood. Slowly she approached him.

"I thought this would be cozier."

"I don't do cozy, Tristan."

"Really?"

In a single motion she popped open the snaps of her lemon yellow faux-suede dress and let it fall to the floor.

"What the hell . . ." His head spun toward the open door. Voices drew close. His mind raced through all the scenarios if someone should walk by and see her standing there half naked. Instinct and self preservation made him shut the door.

Tristan smiled seductively and took a step closer.

Blake held up his palm. "Don't."

She grabbed his hand and took one of his fingers into her mouth.

He tugged his hand away. "This has got to stop." He glared at her. "Get dressed and get out of my office." He turned to leave. She rushed and placed herself between him and the door. Her body was flush up against him.

"You know you want me," she whispered. Her chest heaved in and out. "I want you and I always have from the first moment I saw you." She snatched a handful of his shirt in her fist. "Your wife will never have to know."

Her scent was all around him. Her lips a breath away from his.

She reached between them and unsnapped the front of her bra. Her breasts spilled out.

Blake groaned deep in his throat. Savannah's face wafted before him.

He grabbed Tristan by her shoulders and forcibly moved her out of the way. He yanked the door open and glared at her.

"The next time I walk into my office, I don't want to find you here. And the hell with your company, the deal and anything else you want to toss at me. You're not worth it."

He slammed the door and stormed down the hallway to the men's room. Thankfully it was empty. He went to the sink and splashed cold water on his face. His heart was pumping like crazy. He braced his palms on the sink and drew in long deep breaths. Fury pounded in his temples.

Blake ran a hand across his face. He knew Tristan was bold but never did he expect her to pull something like that. Suppose someone would have walked in. His jaw clenched.

Tomorrow he would set up a meeting with his lawyers and see if there was any way he could break the contract. His shoulders suddenly sagged. What about the company? His employees? The future of his business?

He looked at his reflection in the mirror. No matter what was at stake, he'd never be able to face himself or Savannah if he slept with Tristan. Never.

He straightened his shirt and walked out. He went directly to the front desk.

"Did Ms. Montgomery leave?" he asked Jasmine.

"Yes, a few minutes ago. Is everything okay? She was furious. She looked like she was crying."

Blake blinked back his surprise. "I have no idea. Maybe she got an upsetting phone call. Listen, I'm heading home."

"Did Steven tell you about his brother?"

"Yes. I'm going to see if I can get any more details. If I hear anything before the end of the day, I'll call so that you can inform the staff."

Jasmine nodded her head.

Blake returned to his office, grabbed his briefcase, turned off his computer and headed out. He needed to see Savannah.

Savannah got out of her dress and tossed it on the bed, then kicked off her shoes. Blake wouldn't be home for a couple of hours. That would give her plenty of time to check the devices.

She sat on the edge of the bed and pulled her laptop to her, booted it up and waited. After logging in, she went to the TLC database and punched in her codes and turned up her speakers. After several key-strokes she saw the audio grid appear on her screen with an indication that it was location one, Tristan's home.

Her pulse rate accelerated. She could hear the housekeepers talking. A smile bloomed. She'd done it. She set the audio to Record, then entered the codes necessary to access audio and video from Tristan's office. After several moments, a grainy picture of Tristan's office appeared on her screen. The room, from what Savannah could tell, was empty. She adjusted the sound quality and set the audio to Record.

She sat back and took a shaky breath. There was no telling what she would see or hear in the coming days, but her gut instinct told her it would be well worth the wait.

Now that everything was set, she synched her PDA to the activated signals. This would give her access to anything that came through whenever she was away from her laptop.

She shut down her computer and put it away. The last thing she needed at this point was to be careless and have Blake stumble across what she was doing.

Her stomach tightened. Blake. She tried to push to the back of her mind images of him and Tristan. She didn't want what she felt to be true. One way or the other she would find out — her way.

She returned her laptop to the upper shelf of her closet then went to take a shower.

CHAPTER 18

Blake arrived at Savannah's office, the need to see and speak with his wife overpowering. On the drive over he'd decided that he was going to tell Savannah everything — the kiss, the threats and Tristan's performance today in his office. Together they would decide what to do.

He pushed through the glass doors and ran into Richard.

"Blake. This is a surprise. What brings you here?"

"I wanted to surprise Savannah."

"Oh." He frowned. "Savannah left several hours ago. Said something came up and she darted out. Is everything all right?"

Blake was stumped for a moment. "I . . . Did she say what it was?"

"No, she didn't."

"Thanks." He flashed a sheepish grin. "I guess the surprise is on me. I'll catch her at home. Take it easy, Richard."

"Yeah, you, too," he said to Blake's retreating back.

The minute he got into his car he called Savannah on her cell phone. After several rings it went straight to voice mail. He left a short message asking her to call him then disconnected the call.

For a few minutes he sat in the car trying to think what could have come up that had her dashing out of the office. He put the car in gear and headed home.

Savannah stepped out of the steamy bathroom, feeling a bit better. After she'd activated all the listening devices she'd suddenly felt dirty — peeking into someone else's personal life. It was such a violation of privacy. But then she thought about her assignment and her marriage. Feeling a little dirty was worth it and nothing that a little hot water and soap wouldn't cure.

She was just putting on her robe when the phone rang. Caller ID indicated that it was her mother.

"Hey, Mom."

"Did I ever tell you how much I dislike caller ID?" was her response.

Savannah laughed. "It has its perks. How are you?"

"Fine."

"I called your office and the secretary said you left early. Is everything okay?"

"Everything is fine, Mom."

"Did I ever tell you that as much as I dislike caller ID, I dislike you lying to me even more?"

Savannah pushed out a breath and strolled back into the bathroom. She'd wanted to spill what had been weighing so heavily on her heart to someone. She'd hinted at it with the girls and their response was not what she'd wanted to hear.

"What is it, Savannah? The assignment? Blake? Are you ill?"

There was a long pause before she finally responded. "A combination of all three," she confessed.

"Talk to me, sweetheart."

Savannah sat on the side of the tub and slowly began to tell her mother what had happened; the blatant lie that Blake told, how she was still torn about the assignment that could possibly implicate Blake, her fear of losing him to Tristan.

Claudia listened with an open heart and an open mind. She knew her daughter. Savannah was loyal to a fault, but when she felt slighted or betrayed she could be vengeful. She'd been like that since she was a little girl. She'd seen Savannah cut off her friends for the slightest infraction of trust. And she knew that as much as Savannah loved Blake she would slice him off at the knees if she discovered what she believed to be true. But Claudia also knew that one of Savannah's biggest faults was her sometimes lack of confidence in herself, not so much her abilities, but her looks. Savannah always felt she didn't measure up in the looks department when compared with other women. And if Tristan Montgomery even slightly resembled her photographs, Savannah was probably tied in knots.

"Honey, you listen and you listen to me good. Blake loves you. I'm sorry that the very first assignment from the Cartel had to involve him. But, no matter what, you must not reveal anything about the organization to him. Ever."

"I know that but —"

"No buts. Do your job and believe in your husband. I'm sure there is an explanation for the perfume."

"But he lied to me. How am I supposed to deal with that? How can I trust him after that or believe anything he has to say?"

"He very well may have had a reason. And you can sort it all out when the job is finished."

"But suppose . . ."

"Get all of the ugly pictures out of your head and stay focused. What have you found out so far?"

"I've set the listening devices in her home and office. . . ."

Blake stood on the other side of the bathroom door, frozen.

"I have a little more than a week to collect the evidence I need before the groundbreaking."

He couldn't make sense of what she was saying. Listening devices? The groundbreaking?

He caught a glimpse of the dress on the bed. He walked over and picked it up. The tag was still inside but he could tell it had been worn. What the hell was going on?

"I've got to go. I'll keep you posted. Love you, too." She turned to leave the bathroom and stopped cold.

Tristan stormed into her town house. Fury boiled in her veins. How dare he turn her down? Who in the hell did he think he was? He was nobody that's who he was.

She tossed her purse on the hall table and stomped into her bedroom. Suddenly, she didn't feel so tough anymore. She was hurt, humiliated. Hot tears burned her eyes. She plopped down on her bed just as her phone rang.

She snatched up the phone. "Yes?"

"Hey, Tristan. It's Cynthia."

Tristan drew herself up. Cynthia Harrington was her closest friend and biggest competitor. Since they were kids growing up on Long Island they had been in constant competition with each other, from clothes to cars to men — always trying to outdo the other.

"Hi, Cynthia. How are you?"

"Good. Calling to see what you're up to and to get all the juicy details on Mr. Fields."

Tristan squeezed her eyes shut. She'd never hear the end of it if she told Cynthia the truth — that Blake had turned down her advances.

"Everything is going according to plan and right on schedule."

"Really? Tell, tell. How and when?"

Tristan wove a tale fit for the raciest romance novel up to and including her fabricated session in Blake's office hours earlier.

"What! You seduced him right in his own office?"

"Right on the desk, the floor." She laughed. "It was fabulous. He was fabulous.

Just like I knew he'd be."

"I have to hand it to you, when you set your sights on something it's a done deal. So now what? What about his wife?"

"It's like I told him, she never has to know. And she won't. Unless I decide otherwise." She sputtered a nasty chuckle.

They talked some more and Tristan finally begged off, complaining of needing to sit in a hot tub to massage her aching body after being with Blake.

She hung up the phone, disgusted with her lie but more disgusted that it wasn't true.

CHAPTER 19

"Blake . . . I didn't hear you come in." She pulled her robe closed.

He stared at her for a moment. "Left work early. I stopped by your job."

Her heart thumped.

"Ran into Richard. He said something came up and you rushed out."

"Uh, yes." She forced a smile and brushed by him.

"So . . . what happened?"

She kept her back to him, noticed the flashing light on her PDA that was sitting on the nightstand.

"I . . . Nia and I are planning a surprise party for Dani. I had some running around to do. That's all."

"Really? That's the reason for the dress?"

Her eyes darted to the dress still on the bed. Inwardly, she groaned. "Yes. I went to Neiman Marcus and bought it today. It's going to be a dressy affair."

"And what are you ladies celebrating?"

"She, uh, just landed a major new client and we wanted to celebrate. Just the girls. You know."

She finally turned to him. "What made you come up to my office?"

It was on the tip of his tongue to tell her everything, the turmoil he felt, the decisions he wasn't sure if he could make. But suddenly, he didn't know who she was.

"Had an urge to see you, that's all. And I wanted to tell you about Steven. His brother was in an accident."

Her eyes widened in alarm. "Oh, no. Is Carl okay?"

"I'm not sure." He crossed the room. "I'm going to call Steven shortly and find out." He walked to his dresser then turned to face her. "You want to tell me what's really going on, Savannah?"

"I don't know what you mean."

"How about starting with listening devices?" His gaze zeroed in on her. She didn't flinch.

Savannah felt her stomach drop to her knees. Dammit. She had to think fast. "If you must know . . . and I really shouldn't be telling you this . . . it's an ugly divorce case that Richard has me working on."

He leaned against the dresser and stared

at her. "Richard has you working on a case and planting listening devices?" he asked, his voice laced with disbelief.

She planted her hands on her hips. "Yes. Why is that so hard to believe?"

"Since when does Billings and Tate handle divorces and why in heavens name would they have *you* planting devices instead of a P.I.?"

She swallowed. "I asked to do it," she said, the lie flowing as smooth as melted butter. "And we do handle divorces . . . indirectly. This client is a major corporate executive. He wants to get something on his wife to ensure that she won't take his company."

Blake slung his hands into his pockets. He gave a short shake of his head, not knowing whether to swallow the story whole or to laugh.

"So now you're what . . . some kind of spy?"

Her eye twitched. "Of course not! I convinced Richard that I could get close enough without being someone that she would suspect."

Blake held up his hand. "Enough! Okay. Why are you lying to me? I heard you. You can tell whoever it was on the phone the truth but not me?"

No matter what, you must never reveal what

186

we do. The warning rang in her head.

She spun away. "You're right. I am lying." She walked out of the room. Blake was hot on her heels.

"Savannah. Who is it that you love?"

She nearly tripped over her own feet.

"I heard you tell whoever you were talking to that you loved them, too. Is that the reason for the new dress, for leaving work early, for lying to my face?"

She whirled around. "How dare you?" Her chest heaved in and out. She glared at him. *Don't do it, Savannah,* came the warning. Her thoughts raced. Maybe it would do him some good to feel as crappy as she'd been feeling lately. "Think whatever you want, Blake. If you believe that something is going on, then . . . then maybe we don't have what I thought we did." She brushed by him and headed back to the bedroom. She rifled through her closet and drawers in search of something to put on.

"What are you doing?"

"Getting out of here," she snapped, pulling on a pair of jeans. She tugged a T-shirt over her head.

"Going to meet him!"

She snatched a look at him, stormed past him and snatched her PDA up from the nightstand.

"Don't walk out of here, Savannah. We need to talk."

"Not when you're in this frame of mind." She had to get out of there.

"If you leave, Savannah, I won't be here when you get back."

She halted her steps for an instant. She'd make this right when everything was done, when she had the information she needed. And either she and Blake would weather the storm, or they wouldn't.

"That's your choice, Blake." She picked up her purse and car keys and walked out.

By the time she reached her car and got behind the wheel she was shaking like a leaf. What in the world had she done? What if she was totally wrong about Blake and Tristan? She'd jeopardized her marriage.

But then she thought about his lie — the perfume on his shirt, the same perfume that Tristan wore. If he would lie about something that, what other stories would he tell her? She still gripped her PDA. She looked at it, opened the file and stuck in her headset. Her head began to spin. The contents of her stomach rose to her throat. What she heard pulled the last brick of foundation right out from under her.

Blake was beside himself. What had just

happened? Had Savannah walked out on him, on their marriage? Was she really involved with someone else?

Nothing made sense. The only thing that did was going after her and settling this once and for all. He should never have let her leave. He dashed out of the house and ran down the stairs just as Savannah's SUV tore off from the curb.

CHAPTER 20

Nia was just settling in front of the television when her downstairs doorbell rang. She took off her glasses, pulled herself up from the couch and went to her intercom.

"Who?"

"It's me," a weak voice answered.

Nia frowned and buzzed the door. She was waiting for Savannah when she came upstairs.

"Anna, what is it?"

Savannah walked by her like a ghost.

Nia shut the door and followed Savannah inside. "What's wrong?"

Savannah turned to her friend and Nia's mouth dropped open. She rushed to her and cupped her face in her hands. Her eyes ran over Savannah's face. "What happened?" She bit out the two words.

Savannah's shoulders began to shake and the tears rolled down her cheeks in an unending stream. Her body shuddered and the wretched pain of her sobs pierced Nia's heart. She wrapped Savannah in her arms and held her close, whispering soothing words of comfort.

"Let it out. It's okay."

Savannah held on as an overboard passenger hangs on to a life raft.

Nia ushered Savannah into the living room and eased her down into a chair, never letting her go.

Savannah cried until she had nothing left but dry heaving sobs.

Nia had no idea what was wrong, but she knew it was bad. She'd never seen Savannah like this. They'd always wept on each other's shoulders at one time or the other, but never like this, never this kind of anguish. Everything in her wanted to make Savannah talk, but she knew it would be fruitless until Savannah was ready. Nia being Nia did was she always did during a crisis . . .

"I'm going to fix us something to nibble on. We'll relax, break out a bottle of wine and . . ."

Savannah lifted her head from Nia's shoulder. Her wide dark eyes filled with hurt. "I left him, Nia. I walked out on Blake, on my marriage."

Nia couldn't respond. She thought of the

restaurant, of Dani's photographs, Savannah's story about the perfume. Still, she couldn't believe it had come to this.

"Anna, honey, I'm going to call Dani. Okay?"

Savannah nodded.

Nia got up and went to the phone. When Dani answered Nia could instantly tell that she was otherwise engaged.

"Dani, kick him to the curb," she said instead of hello. "Anna needs us. It's bad. Come to my place, now."

By the time Dani arrived Savannah's sobs had dissipated to silent whimpers. Nia scrunched her face in confusion, looking to Nia for information.

Nia eased up from the couch and pulled Dani into the kitchen.

"What the hell is going on? What happened to her?" Dani hissed through her teeth so as not to be overheard.

"She hasn't said a word other than 'I left him.' "

"What? She left Blake?" her voice snapped in stunned disbelief.

"That's all she said. I was waiting for you before I started asking any questions so that she wouldn't have to go through it more than once."

Dani's head cocked to one side, her right

brow arched and her hand went straight to her hip. "I swear, if that man hurt her, I don't care how fine he is, it's gonna be me and him."

Nia put her hand on Dani's shoulder. "We don't know what happened, so relax until we do. I don't need you going in there in one of your rages."

Dani was infamous for "going off" as she put it. Her tough-girl attitude came from her years of growing up in one of the toughest projects in Brooklyn, walking the treacherous streets to school and circumnavigating the dangerous stairwells of her building. She'd made it out in one piece but many of her childhood friends did not, having succumbed to drugs, gangs, jail or worse. She promised herself that if she ever made it out she would create a world of beauty all around her, which led to her profession as a fashion photographer. She never wanted to see anything ugly again. Nonetheless, old habits die hard and she may have left the projects behind but it was still in her blood.

Dani rolled her eyes. "Okay. I'll be cool. But —" she wagged a warning finger "— if Savannah even breathes that he hurt her . . ."

Nia took her arm. "Come on. And just relax, hear her out."

They returned to the living room. Savannah looked at her friends with swollen eyes. She could tell by Dani's stance that she was ready to do battle and Nia would go along for the ride. Savannah inhaled deeply.

"Since we're all here," she began, "I guess I should tell you what's going on, huh?"

"Whenever you feel like talking, sweetie," Nia said gently.

Dani sat on one side of Savannah and Nia on the other.

"I'm going to tell you something that I've been sworn not to divulge to anyone. It's going to sound crazy, but just hear me out."

They both frowned.

Savannah drew in a breath and slowly laid out her incredible story from the time she was recruited by her mother up to her listening to the recording. When she was finished nearly an hour later, a pin could be heard falling onto Nia's thick carpet.

"Wait . . . let me get this straight," Nia finally said. "You work for some kind of secret agency and you were assigned to spy on Tristan Montgomery?"

Savannah nodded.

"And while you're spying you find out about her and Blake?" Dani asked.

Savannah nodded again. She tugged on her bottom lip with her teeth, suddenly uncertain whether she should have told them anything. But these were her dearest friends. They would never betray her.

"Damn," Dani whispered.

"Double damn," Nia added. "Honey, I'm so sorry. I don't even know what to say."

"I know what to say," Dani said. "Brother needs a beat down and sister girl, too!"

"That's not going to solve anything," Nia said.

"Maybe not, but it would make me feel better."

Savannah gave a weak smile. "I appreciate the sentiment, but Nia is right."

"I want to get back to this secret-agent thing," Dani said. "I'm still trying to wrap my mind around it."

"I've been part of the Cartel for over a year now. This was my first assignment."

Nia shook her head slowly. "Unreal." She paused and looked at Savannah. "So, uh, other than listening equipment, what other tricks of the trade do you have?"

"A PDA that links to computers, tracking devices, software programs to tap into secure Web sites and e-mails, mini video cameras . . . a gun."

Their eyes widened. "Get out!" they said in unison.

Savannah slowly nodded. "But now I'm

wishing I didn't have any of it. This was the biggest mistake I've ever made."

Dani slipped her arm around Savannah's shoulder. "Look, I'm all for kicking a no good man to the curb, but as much as this rubs me the wrong way, I have my doubts."

"Doubts! Were you not listening to Savannah and what she heard on the tape?"

"I know, I know," Dani said, "but I'm a photographer."

"No kidding," Nia cut in.

"Just hear me out. My business is making something out of nothing. I know all about doctoring photos to create a specific impression."

"What are you getting at?" Savannah asked, with an inkling of hope in her voice.

"I'm just saying that life has taught me that most things are not what they seem."

"But I heard it," Savannah insisted.

"Or you heard what she wanted you to hear. What if Blake is totally the innocent one here and Ms. Girl was just running off at the mouth with her friend?"

"But the perfume? What about that?" Savannah asked.

"That could be anything. Maybe she was all up against him and he didn't know how to tell you."

"I can't believe I'm hearing this from

you," Nia said, sincerely surprised. "A minute ago you were ready for a beat down."

Dani grinned. "That was my hothead talking." She turned to face Savannah. "The truth is, I honestly believe that Blake loves you. I don't think he would risk his marriage over a fling. There has to be something else to it."

"Like what?"

Dani was quiet for a moment. "Like I don't know . . . but something."

"So what are you suggesting?" Nia asked.

Dani looked from Nia to Savannah. "I was thinking that even though you said you had the resources of the Cartel at your service, if, and I say if, Blake is up to something it's not a situation that you would want strangers to find out about. Right? Not even your mother."

Savannah's brows drew together. "True," she admitted.

"That's why I think that you should let me and Nia be part of the 'auxiliary' cartel. . . ."

CHAPTER 21

He'd waited long enough. It had been nearly three hours since Savannah had stormed out of the house. His first instinct was to go after her, but then thought it best to let her cool off. She should be icy cold by now and the waiting and not knowing were making him crazy.

In all the years of their marriage nothing like this had ever happened. Sure, they'd had their share of disagreements, as any married couple did. But they'd never walked out on each other, never shut down communication.

If he was honest with himself, he knew that he was the source of the problem between them now. It was his own conscience that caused him to accuse Savannah. She didn't deserve that.

Sitting here wasn't getting the job done. He had to find her, tell her how sorry he was and then try to explain.

He went to the dresser and snatched up his car keys. The only places he could think of were either Dani's or Nia's house or Savannah's mother's. He certainly didn't want to show up on Claudia's doorstep, looking for Savannah. He'd never hear the end of it, no matter how things turned out.

Just as he was heading out of the bedroom, he heard the front door open. He rushed out.

Savannah walked in, looking a little frayed around the edges and her eyes spoke volumes. She'd been crying.

"Baby, listen, I'm sorry." Slowly he approached, unsure of her reaction.

Her eyes held his. "So am I." She pushed out a breath. "We need to talk." She put down her purse and came toward him. She looked up at him, trying to see beyond the idealized image she had of him — her knight in shining armor. "I'm going to ask you something, and I need you to tell me the truth, Blake, no matter what."

His heart thumped. "Of course."

"Do you love me? I mean, really love me?" Her gaze bore into him.

"Savannah . . ." He clasped her shoulders. "I've always loved you." His eyes ran over her face, taking in every detail. "I love you now and tomorrow and the day after, for as

199

long as I can see my future I will love you." He pulled her to him. "I'm in love with you, from the depths of my soul."

Savannah sunk into his embrace, listened to the beating of his heart that pulsed in perfect rhythm with her own, felt the depth of his feelings for her in every breath he took. Whatever happened between him and Tristan, she could not believe it was of his doing. She understood that now as never before.

She tilted her head back and looked at him, the anguish in his eyes, the questions there pierced her heart. She desperately wanted to tell him what she'd been assigned to do. But still, she couldn't. Not yet.

"Then tell me why Tristan's perfume was all over your clothes," she said in a soft, even tone.

Slowly, Blake nodded his head. "She came to my office as she usually does, unexpected." He stepped back and released her, slid his hands into his pants pockets. He leaned against the wall, looking suddenly young and terribly vulnerable.

Savannah held her breath and waited.

He recounted to her what had transpired. She watched every expression that drifted across his face; from stunned surprise to disgust.

"It just came out of nowhere. She kissed me."

A knot formed in Savannah chest. "Did . . . you kiss her back?"

His brows flicked. "It happened so fast I don't even know." He looked straight at her. "I may have. That's the thing that's been eating at me. She was all over me like a heat wave."

Savannah drew in a breath. "So . . . what happened?"

"I put her out."

Savannah turned away and went to sit on the side of the bed.

"There's more."

Her head shot up toward him. The air seemed to get sucked out of her lungs. Please, God, no . . .

"Today we had another meeting, a scheduled one." He shifted his weight from one leg to the other. "Steve and I were supposed to meet with her together so that there wouldn't be any more incidents."

"Steve knows?"

Blake nodded.

Savannah shook her head. The old boy's network, she mused. "Go ahead, I'm listening."

"Well, just before we were getting ready to meet, Steven stopped me on the hallway to tell me about Carl." He swallowed. "So I went in to meet her alone."

Savannah's hands clenched.

"When I got to the conference room she wasn't there. I waited. After about fifteen minutes I figured she left." He paused. "She hadn't. When I went back to my office, she was there."

Telling his wife what happened next was the hardest thing he'd ever had to do, but he needed to get it out, all of it.

Savannah listened in shock. This woman was that bold, that brazen as to out and out seduce her husband in his own office! Her husband! She continued to listen, seething inside. All she wanted to do at that very moment was to snatch Tristan by her hair.

"She's threatened to pull the project away from the company if I don't sleep with her," he finally said, his chest deflating once the words were finally out.

"She what?"

Blake nodded. "She's said it more than once. I told her to go ahead. She swore she would ruin me, ruin the company."

"Why didn't you tell me? You've been dealing with this alone."

"I thought she was bluffing until today."

Savannah's mind was running in circles. This woman so desperately wanted her husband that she was threatening to ruin his business to get her way. If she was capable of that, then she was capable of anything.

"We can't let that happen," she was finally able to say. "You worked too hard. Everyone did. She's not going to ruin that for you, for any of them."

He looked at her with a half smirk. "Great minds think alike." He finally dared to sit next to her. "I didn't want any of this to touch you. But there would have been no way to keep if from you if she went through with her threat. Money and power can do just about anything. If she set her mind to it, I may never be able to work again and I have a staff with families to think about."

"I may as well tell you now," she said.

"What? Don't tell me Richard has been making moves on you?" he said half joking.

Savannah snickered. "No. Nothing like that. I — uh, went to see Tristan today."

His neck jerked back. "Why?"

"Insecurity."

"Insecurity? What are you talking about?"

She glanced over her shoulder toward the dress on the bed. "That was the reason for the dress. I wanted her to see me as fabulous as she is." She swallowed. "Ever since I met her at the party and realized she wore the same perfume I'd smelled on you and then you denied it . . . I felt . . . hurt and confused and I thought that I might lose you to her."

"Savannah, baby, you can't lose me. It's not possible." He took her hand. "And why in the world would you feel insecure?"

She pushed up from the bed. "I've always felt that way," she said almost to herself. "Especially around beautiful women." She turned to face him. "I know I'm no beauty queen, I never have been." She held up her hand as he opened his mouth. "I know, I'm beautiful to you. But, the truth is, I'm short. I can get overweight just thinking about food and if I didn't go to the salon every week I could be a cover model for *Fright Digest.* But, as I always tell myself, I clean up good." She sputtered a self-deprecating laugh. "But up against someone like Tristan, who is naturally beautiful, rich and powerful, I felt totally inadequate. And I wanted to at least level the playing field when I went to see her." She lowered her head focusing on the pattern of the rug. "And I thought there was something going on between you, and it was killing me inside."

The next thing she knew her feet were off the floor and she was up in Blake's muscular arms. He cradled her against him and walked to the bed, putting her down like a fine piece of china. He leaned over her.

He unbuttoned her blouse and peeled it away. Her breasts, rapidly, rose and fell. He slid her drawstring sweatpants down over her hips and pulled them off. He reached behind her and unhooked her bra, pulled it off and tossed it on the floor. His dark, hungry gaze ran up and down her body, setting every inch on fire.

Then suddenly he took her hands and pulled her to her feet. "Come." He took her across the room, opened the closet and stood her in front of the full-length mirror, with him behind her.

"You want to know what I see when I look at you?"

She pressed her lips together to keep from crying.

"I see silky smooth brown skin that feels like satin beneath my fingertips. I see warmth and heat and sparkle in your brown eyes and a hint of mischief. I love the way they turn slightly up at the end and the sweep of your brows that crinkle when you're deep in thought. And your mouth, it's full and rich and so very kissable. Your high cheekbones speak to your ancestry and make me remember from where we came." His hands trailed down to her waist and held her. "I can put my hands around your waist and feel my fingers curve out to your delicious hips. And those thighs, they're strong and tight and hug me when I make love with you." His hands rose upward and cupped the weight of her breasts in his palms. "These are a work of art, perfect in every way," he whispered.

He turned her around to face him and saw the tears sparkling in her eyes. "Yeah, you're not tall enough to be a runway model, but you're just right for me. You make me feel powerful and strong and longing to protect you." He tilted her face up with the tip of his fingers. "But most of all what I see is your spirit, the joy and fullness of it that reaches out and embraces everyone and everything. Love may be blind, but I see you, Savannah Fields. I see all of you, inside and out and I love every bit of you, from the bottom of your tiny feet to the crown of your head. All of you, everyday, always."

The tears came in a steady stream, hanging on the corners of her mouth before falling onto Blake's hand. He wiped them away with the pads of his thumbs.

"I want you to finally see yourself as I see you," he said with so much tenderness a new wave of tears fell down to her cheeks. "And I promise no more secrets between us, no matter what. We're a team."

A pang of guilt mixed with the pangs of love she felt for Blake. She desperately wanted to tell him everything. But she couldn't. She wrapped her arms around him, held him as tight as she could, never wanting to let him go, let the ugliness of the world get in between them.

In unison, reading each other's need they moved toward the bed. They lay next to each other, touching, sharing featherlight kisses, heating their bodies by leaping degrees. Savannah moaned against Blake's mouth.

He turned her onto her back, suckled her neck until he could feel her entire body shudder. He whispered hot words of love and desire deep into her ear while his hands electrified her skin.

Every place he touched caught on fire. Her pulse sounded like a tidal wave in her ears.

Blake pushed his hand between their bodies, found her center wet and pulsing. Savannah squirmed, pushed her pelvis against his hand.

One finger slid inside of her. Savannah whimpered.

"Blake," she cried out in a rush of air.

"I know," he said in a hushed voice before

easing deep inside her. "I love you, too."

As she lay curled next to her husband, comforted by the security of his embrace she felt a hard knot of guilt. Sex and lies. They'd become all tangled together. Still, much of what she told Blake was true. She'd left out only part of the reason *why* she went to see Tristan. She was more determined than ever to get the goods on her. And now she had the help of her two best friends.

CHAPTER 22

Blake jumped up with a start about an hour later. He'd never gotten around to calling Steven to check on Carl. He cursed under his breath and eased out of bed trying not to disturb Savannah. He tiptoed out of the bedroom and went up front to use the phone.

After several rings Steven picked up his cell.

"Hey, man, I know it's late," Blake said. "It's been a crazy day. How is Carl?"

"The doctors say he's going to be fine. He has a concussion, a broken leg and a cracked rib."

Blake leaned against the fridge and expelled a breath of relief. "That's great news. It could have been worse. I know you must be feeling a hundred percent better."

"Definitely." He yawned. "We're just getting in from the hospital. He'll be in about a week and then they plan to send him

209

home. I'm gonna take a few days off and stay here with my sister-in-law. Seems like no matter what the docs say she's still worried. I don't want her to be alone and with the kids, too."

"Hey, no problem, do what you have to for your family, just keep me posted."

"Hang on a sec. Let me grab a beer then you can tell me how the meeting went."

Blake hung on and decided to raid the fridge while he waited.

Savannah felt and heard Blake leave the bedroom. She got out of bed and went to the door. He was on the phone in the kitchen. More than likely he was talking with Steve, she surmised. If that was the case that would give her a few minutes to check the recordings from Tristan's office and home. Steve and Blake were notorious for lengthy conversations.

She got her PDA and her headset from her purse then returned to the bed. After turning it on, she surfed to the secure Web site and keyed in her code which would upload the recorded files that she needed. The two-inch screen displayed an audio box in full color complete with sound levels. She put on her headset and within minutes was listening to conversations in Tristan's office.

Most were basic business conversations, a call to what sounded like her hairstylist, another to her masseuse.

Savannah rolled her eyes as she listened to the drivel and wondered how in the world this woman could run a major empire when the bulk of her time was taken up with hair and nail appointments, massages and trying to seduce other women's husbands. She was just about to turn it off, when she hit pay dirt. She turned up the volume and listened intently.

"I don't give a damn about the regulations, Larry. I told you what needed to be done with the project. I'm not going to have some paper-pushing lackey tell me when I can build, where and on what. Make it go away. This has got to go on schedule as planned. The groundbreaking is next week."

"Tristan, at some point this is going to be discovered. And when it does all hell is going to break loose."

"All the more reason why you need to make it go away. Pay them whatever it takes, but this project starts on time. Too much is riding on it."

"I'll see what can be done."

"Don't see, do. Goodbye, Larry and don't call back unless you have good news."

The call disconnected. Who was Larry,

and what did Tristan want to go away?

Savannah glanced up and saw Blake's shadow moving toward the bedroom. She quickly took off the earbuds and popped the PDA in the nightstand drawer just as he walked in.

He grinned when he saw her. "You're up." He took another bite of his overstuffed turkey sandwich.

Savannah smiled and slowly shook her head in amazement. Blake was blessed with a metabolism that burned off food almost as soon as he ate it. He could gobble down anything he wanted day or night and still stayed lean and muscular. She was sure his once or twice a week workout helped but nothing beats good genes.

He ambled over to the bed. "I didn't mean to wake you." He held out the sandwich toward her. "Want a bite?"

Her stomach yelled yes. But she knew better. "No, thanks. I'll get some water."

"I talked to Steve."

She placed a hand on his forearm. "How is Carl?"

He relayed the conversation.

"Thank God for that."

"He's going to take some time off and stay out there at least until Carl comes home, maybe a bit longer."

Savannah nodded. "Are you going to be able to manage the office and the projects without him?"

"Yeah, we worked it all out over the phone. He has his laptop and his Black-Berry. We'll stay in touch. If necessary we can video-teleconference any major meeting." The corner of his mouth quirked up into a grin. "Technology. Humph." He chewed on the last of his sandwich. "You can do just about anything these days with all the gadgets."

No kidding, Savannah thought as Blake slid back in bed. No kidding.

"So how are we going to do this?" Dani asked Nia as she munched on a croissant with jelly.

They were seated inside their favorite coffee and bagel spot down in Tribeca a few blocks from the Borough of Manhattan Community College, off Chambers Street. Even though this little eatery was in the heart of where the World Trade Center once stood, miraculously it hadn't sustained a scratch during the 9/11 attack. If anything, once life in lower Manhattan returned to seminormal, it had become even more of an attraction. It was additionally convenient for both Dani and Nia as their respective offices were walking distance in either direction. At any given time one star or the other would saunter into the shop trying to blend in with the crowd. But Dani's eagle photographic eye always caught them all. Kevin Bacon, De Niro, Spike, the author Bernice McFadden, Gwyneth Paltrow, even Brad and Angie have popped in with their brood in tow.

But the one day that had them both on the floor, practically under the table, was when Denzel Washington strolled in with a black baseball cap pulled down low over his brow, baggy jeans, sneakers and wearing a black windbreaker. He may have gone totally unnoticed but Dani could spot that signature Denzel walk in the dark and blindfolded. But by the time they'd both pulled themselves together he was gliding out of the door. They still laughed about how they'd sat there with their mouths hanging open unable to move.

Nia lifted the cup of green tea to her lips and took a sip. "Well, Savannah has Tristan covered. So any funny business and she'll be the first to know."

"Uh-huh."

"So I think our focus should be on the location. And watching Tristan's comings and goings, who she's with, stuff like that."

"I can take care of that. You handle the location."

Nia agreed. "I'm going to check into everyone involved with the project. You've got Tristan's movements covered and Savannah takes care of video and audio."

"Between the three of us we'll be able to nail her." Dani slapped her palm on the table, causing a few heads to turn in their direction. She cut her eyes from side to side. "Sorry," she muttered. "One thing we left out. Tristan's friend, the chick she was talking to on the phone."

"What about her?"

"We need to find out who she is, where she hangs out. Maybe Ms. Montgomery confided more than a few lies to her." She raised her brows to make her point.

Nia slowly nodded her head in agreement. "I'll take care of it."

"Good." Dani checked her watch. "I've got to run. I have a photo shoot in midtown at noon. I need to meet my crew in like twenty minutes." She scrambled out of the booth, grabbed her backpack and snatched up her car keys from the table. She bent down and planted a quick kiss on Nia's cheek. "See you later. Double 0."

Nia giggled at the James Bond reference and swatted Dani's arm. "Guess I'm paying, huh?"

"Guess so." Dani hummed to herself as she dashed out.

Nia took her purse from beside her, fished around inside and took her out her eyeglass case, took a quick look around and slipped on her glasses. She flipped open her electronic address book.

In the years that she'd been in the event-planning business, she'd made it her duty and the duty of everyone that worked for her to take names and numbers from busboys to corporate CEOs. Her list was legendary in the business. Everyone knew that if you wanted to find someone, Nia Turner had the number.

She scrolled through her database and found the info for Desmond Reynolds. Desi, as his friends called him, of which Nia was a close one. He knew everything there was to know about New York City history. She wanted to find out all that she could about the construction site in Brooklyn. She highlighted his name and all his info came up from his private cell number to his shoe size. She scrolled for his number then punched it into her BlackBerry.

"You've reached my voice mail. What a shame. However, leave me a message with your name and number and if I choose, I'll call you back. Ciao."

"Hey, Desi. This is Nia Turner. I really need to pick your brain and soon. Give me a call as soon as possible. It's important." She left both her cell phone and home number before hanging up.

She'd packed up her gadgets and tucked her glasses away, just as her BlackBerry chimed. Desi's name and number showed in the illuminated display.

"Thanks for getting back so quickly," she said in greeting.

"Anything for you, doll. Now, what can I do to enlighten your day?"

"Well . . ."

CHAPTER 23

Savannah arrived at her office feeling much better than she had the day before. She knew she'd broken the cardinal rule of the Ladies Cartel by divulging its existence and purpose to Dani and Nia, but what they'd said as she'd bared her soul hit a chord with her. Would she rather have some outsider looking into her husband and Tristan, or her best friends? She chose friendship over protocol.

What was most troubling, which she hadn't voiced out loud, was the fact that when she was given the assignment Jean had to know who Blake was and that he was her husband.

That fact alone she knew was the ultimate test of her loyalty to the Cartel. But it also gave her even more impetus to clear her husband of any wrongdoing and prove to the Cartel that she could be trusted with any assignment — well, almost trusted.

Savannah tucked her newest Kate Spade purse in her bottom desk drawer, spun her chair toward her computer screen and powered it up.

Each member of the trio had their assignments. Hers was to tap into Tristan's computer.

While her computer loaded her programs, she took out her PDA and connected it to her BlackBerry then she opened her e-mail program. On her PDA she scrolled to the files and found the one she needed. It was a Trojan file that, when sent to an unsuspecting recipient would trace and record every keystroke that was made.

Savannah typed her thank-you note to Tristan.

Dear, Ms. Montgomery,
I can't thank you enough for allowing me to visit your offices. Just as Blake said, it is fabulous. I will certainly be speaking with my boss about upgrading our office space. I am truly inspired.

All best,
Savannah Fields

Normally, it should read "all the best," but the tracking code was embedded in those two words, innocuous enough to be ignored as no more than a typo.

Savannah drew in a breath as she re-read the note. Satisfied, she hit Send from her PDA which sent the signal to the Black-Berry. In an instant her display showed that her message had been sent. Now all she had to do was wait.

"I need a little more light on her face," Dani instructed as she peered through the lens of her camera.

This particular shoot was for one of her big corporate clients — Bergdorf Goodman. She was shooting their winter catalog, which was a feat in and of itself since it was the height of summer in the city and the models were layered down in fur coats, boots and scarves. It was a herculean task to keep the barely there, waiflike models from passing out from heat exhaustion. Her interns had to continually ply them with water.

By two o'clock they called it quits with a check-in time for 10:00 a.m. the following morning.

"Great day today," Nick Touro said as he slung his bag of equipment over his shoulder.

Nick had been with Danielle's International — the name for her business — for a little more than six months. In that time they'd become more than business associates. None of her employees knew they were seeing each other, they made sure of that, which was fine with her. What did tug at her conscience was that she hadn't told the girls and she wasn't sure if it was because of her uncertainty about where the relationship was heading or because Nick was white.

Sure she had some Hispanic blood in her veins on her maternal grandmother's side which accounted for her golden brown complexion and silky ink-black hair. But her dad was black through and through, so therefore she was, as well.

She lived in a black world, grew up with all the stigmas and pressures associated with being a person of color. If anything, because of her mixed heritage and outward looks, it made her more militant, more pro black as if she needed to validate her blackness. The fact that she had fallen for a white guy totally messed with her head and shook up the very foundation upon which she built her life.

Dani stole a look at Nick as they trudged out of the fake winter studio, and her heart thumped just a little in her chest.

What would the girls think? she wondered.

He turned eyes so inky black they were almost be purple in her direction. A dimple dented his left cheek.

"How about dinner later? I was thinking of going to the Lenox Lounge afterward. The Danny Mixon trio is playing tonight."

Dani laughed inwardly. Nick Touro was the blackest white boy she knew. He was more into every phase of black music than she ever was and had a collection that would rival Motown. His favorite food was ribs dripping in sauce with spicy collards and a heaping helping of potato salad. They spent many a Friday or Saturday night at Brothers restaurant on Seventh Avenue South where they specialized in his favorite foods. Sometimes she felt like a discredit to her race when Nick would discuss the politics of Cornell West or Michael Eric Dyson or the inner workings of apartheid in South Africa and the chilling similarities in the States. She felt compelled to bone up on her history here and abroad.

"Then I was hoping I could entreat you to stay at my place tonight. I bought this new massage oil that I'm dying to try out on you," he said as they stood on the corner of Houston Street.

That was the other thing. Sex. Lord, just thinking about sex with Nick made her entire body go on full alert. He held nothing back and took her to sexual heights that you only read about in romance novels. Maybe white men can't jump but this one sure knew how to put it down.

A hot flush raced from her center and flooded her cheeks.

Nick grinned. "Am I embarrassing you?"

"No. Why?" She stammered.

"Because your cheeks are red."

"Oh." She waved her hand to toss the comment aside. "Just hot, that's all."

Nick winked. "That's the way I like you," he said in a whisper.

Perspiration trickled down the center of her back.

"So how about it?" he asked. "We'll make a night of it." His dark eyes bored into her.

"Sure. Love it. What time?"

"I'll pick you up around six. We'll eat then head back uptown then to my place."

Dani smiled, feeling giddy and girlish. "Can't wait," she said, and meant it.

Nick bent down just a bit and kissed her lightly on the lips. "See you later," he said against her mouth.

Her eyes fluttered open. "See ya."

Nick started off down the street toward the train station en route to Gold's Gym, which he frequented at least three times per week.

She'd have to tell the girls about Nick

pretty soon. She knew she couldn't keep how she felt to herself much longer without bursting.

Dani turned and headed toward the garage where her Edge was parked. She checked her watch. Two forty-five. That would give her a few hours to do a bit of eye-spy work on Ms. Tristan Montgomery.

Tristan was crankier than usual when she returned to her office from an off-site meeting.

What had transpired between her and Blake in his office still stabbed deeply at her ego and her womanhood.

She breezed by the receptionists and staffers without a word or even to acknowledge their greetings. Her mind was on Blake Fields and had been since she met him.

Thoughts of Blake plagued her dreams both day and night. She couldn't get him out of her mind, and the desire to make love to him was sometimes so overwhelming that she found herself sneaking off from meetings to find a place to release her pent-up urges. Erotic images of the two of them would wake her from her sleep and she'd find herself trembling and moaning from the orgasm that dreams of Blake would evoke.

It was making her crazy. It drove her to pull that stunt in his office. She'd never been so humiliated in her life or felt that desperate.

Tristan entered her office and shut the door. She drew the blinds over the glass front of her office that faced the corridor. Sighing heavily she took off her suit jacket and dropped it across the couch then went to her desk. Pushing her honey brown hair over her shoulder she turned on her computer and started off by checking her e-mail.

She had forty new messages. She went through each one, replied to the ones that required her immediate attention, forwarded others to her assistant, deleted most and left the others for another time.

She came to one whose e-mail address — sf@billingstate.com — she didn't immediately recognize. She frowned for a moment but since it had no attachments she figured it was safe. She clicked it open, but it took several seconds for the message to appear.

She couldn't have been more surprised or annoyed, she couldn't tell which. It was a note from Savannah, the one thing that stood in the way of her and Blake.

Tristan read the very gracious note, picturing Savannah in her mind and wondered what Blake saw in her. Everything about

Savannah was ordinary, from her height to her hairdo. She just couldn't understand Blake's fascination or, more important, his loyal devotion.

Was that love? Was that what it made you do? Was it so powerful that it would make you risk anything to keep it safe?

Tristan didn't know what that was. What it felt like for someone to feel that way about her. But she wanted it. She wanted to know and experience it. And she wanted it with Blake. Somehow she'd find a way to make him want her just as desperately.

She clicked off Savannah's e-mail without answering.

Her intercom buzzed. She rolled her eyes at the flashing light before responding.

"Yes."

"Mr. Washington is on two."

"Thank you." She picked up the line. "Yes, Larry. Only good news I hope."

"Yes, I'll be over in about a half hour. We'll do a late lunch and talk."

"I'll make reservations at Cipriani's."

"That's why I love dining with you. See you soon."

Tristan hung up, feeling shades better. At least one of her headaches was being dealt with. There was no way that this project could be stopped. Everything was riding on it.

She returned to her e-mail screen and sent a quick note to her driver that he was needed shortly and to be out front in ten minutes.

Then she sent off an e-mail to one of her financiers — Jeffrey Corbin of the Corbin Group.

Dear, Jeff.
Just a quick note to let you know that everything is still on schedule. All of the glitches have been worked out and it's full steam ahead. We're both going to be very happy and very rich.
Best, T.

Dani pulled up in front of Trump Tower and was instantly pounced upon by bellhops and valets.

"I'm just waiting for someone," she said, leaning toward her passenger-side window.

"You can't wait here, ma'am. You're going to have to move down toward the corner or I'd be happy to park your car for you."

She had to think fast. If she pulled too far away she wouldn't be able to see Tristan if she left the building. If she parked her car she'd never get it in time to follow her.

"Please, miss, you're going to have to move your vehicle."

She was just about to call Savannah and check to see if her camera was on Tristan when she spotted her coming out of the building with a man in a gray suit. Tristan put on her shades, walked to the curb just as a black town car pulled up right in front of her. The duo ducked inside.

"Never mind. I guess I'd better go," she said to the flustered valet.

She eased off into traffic and followed the car. Once they were about a block away her cell phone chirped. She pressed her hands-free set.

"Hello?"

"Dani, it's Savannah. I found out that Tristan is meeting Larry and they're going to Cipriani's."

"I'm right behind her car," Dani said with a note of pride in her voice. "At least knowing where they're going will make following them easier in case I lose them."

"Great. See if you can get a picture of this guy. Okay?"

"That's the plan. Hey, call Nia. I'm sure she knows the head somebody in charge over there. See if she can get me a table."

"I'll call you right back."

Dani had watched enough episodes of *Law*

& *Order* to know not to get too close. But just on the off chance that they changed their minds about the restaurant, she didn't want to lag too far behind.

Her cell chirped again.

"Hello?"

"I don't know how she does it, but she got you a reservation."

Dani beamed. She'd been dying to go to Cipriani's.

"Thanks. I'll keep you posted." She disconnected the call and a few moments later the car glided to a stop in front of the famed restaurant.

Dani aimed her telephoto lens at the car and began snapping as the gentleman exited the car and helped Tristan to her feet. She caught him at several angles before they entered the restaurant.

She pulled up front and a valet came and opened her door.

"Welcome to Cipriani's."

"Thank you." She stepped out as regally as the rest of the high-heeled, high-browed guests, glad that she was always attired to go anywhere at any time. She pulled her two-foot silk, leopard-print scarf out of her purse and draped it around her neck, letting it fall over each shoulder. Her black safari shirt dress was perfect with her black peep-toe, sling backed pumps. She slung her black and beige designer signature purse over her shoulder, slid on her black shades and strolled inside looking every bit like a super model.

A hostess greeted her at the door.

"Welcome. The name on your reservation, please?"

"Danielle Holloway."

The hostess tapped some keys on her computer screen then smiled up at Dani.

"Right this way."

Dani scanned the semidark interior looking for signs of Tristan and company. She spotted them up ahead in a booth separated from the one next to it with beveled glass.

The hostess led Dani right past Tristan's table.

"Um, would it be all right if I sat here?" Dani asked pointing to the empty booth opposite Tristan's.

The hostess turned. "Those are for more than one person."

"When the reservation was made the restaurant was informed that it would be for two people."

The young woman looked put out for a minute. "I'm sure there . . ."

"Nia Turner made my reservation." Hopefully Nia's name carried as much weight with the Indians as it did with the chiefs.

The woman's blue eyes widened in delight and a smile stretched across her thin lips.

"Miss Turner! Why didn't you say so? If she took care of you I'm sure it's fine."

Dayum, Dani thought. It does work.

The hostess double backed to the empty booth and helped Dani into her seat. "As soon as your other party arrives, I'll have them seated. Please tell Miss Turner hello for me and that I still love that scarf she sent for my birthday."

Dani smiled. "I'll be sure to tell her." She peered at her name tag. "Jillian."

Once she was gone, Dani opened her menu. Fortunately in a restaurant like this the noise level was more of a hum as opposed to real noise. Dani sat right next to the glass in hopes of catching tidbits of conversation.

With Tristan out of the office and away from home there wasn't much she could do except to wait.

Richard strolled over to her desk. She only hoped that he wasn't in trauma mode.

"Hey, Richard."

"Hi. I need you to go over to the county clerk's office in Brooklyn and pull what you can on this address." He handed her a sheet

231

of paper with a map and a property grid. The address he needed verified was circled in red.

"We're going to need the history of this place — all the owners from as far back as you can dig."

"Okay, what's the case about?"

"Seems that there's been some major discrepancies about who the true owners of the property are. Our clients said that they own it, that it was deeded to them by their great grandmother and they've only discovered the deed. However, the current owners say they have the deed. It is a prime piece of property in Westchester. The value of the house alone is well over three million and that's not including the land value."

"Wow. I'll get right on it. Find out what I can."

"I'm sure it will take the rest of the day, so bring in whatever you find in the morning." He paused. "By the way, is everything all right with you and Blake? He came here looking for you after you left the other day."

She nodded. "Yes, fine. We just got our signals crossed."

Richard looked at her for a moment.

She reached for her purse in the bottom drawer. "I'm, uh, going to head out now. See how much I can accomplish before they close shop for the day."

"Fine, and thanks, Savannah."

"Not a problem." She gathered her things, thankful for the distraction of an assignment to get her mind off of her "other assignment."

After circling the block surrounding the county clerk's office looking for a parking space, she finally gave up and parked in one of the overpriced lots.

Hurrying up the granite steps into the building entrance her cell phone rang. It was Nia.

"I'm not sure what all of this means," she began without even a hello. "But I got some information from my friend Desi. It seems that those rail yards where the development is being constructed have a very interesting history . . ."

Savannah's thoughts were spinning by the time she found the right office to begin her research. If what Desi found out was true, not only were they sitting on a land mine, but the conspiracy to keep it quiet ran all the way up the rung of local government, maybe higher.

Her temples pounded. She was more certain than ever that Blake knew nothing about this. She couldn't imagine that he would have signed on if he had the full story.

The thing now was to prove it and to prove that Tristan Montgomery was complicit in the cover-up.

As she sat in front of the microfiche machine tracing the history of the land in Westchester something suddenly occurred to her.

If someone desperately wanted land that could bring them millions in revenue, how far would they go to make sure that happened?

The case she was working on for Richard was the perfect example. People will do anything for money and money-producing land only sweetened the pot.

Savannah took copious notes. One thing that she always prided herself on was her ability to sift through the fluff of legal documents and get to the facts. In a bit more than an hour she'd gone as far back as 1910 to discover the original owners and traced the progression of the deed right up until the present day. She smiled. Satisfied. Richard would be pleased and so would their client. They had a very nice case against the offenders who'd apparently moved into the home when it became abandoned, rehabbed it and dummied up the ownership documents. There was nothing in the files to indicate that the offenders were the true owners of the building.

She slipped all of the copies and the notes she'd made into a folder just as a wizened clerk came around to say that they were closing in twenty minutes.

Savannah tapped him on the shoulder as he passed.

"Excuse me. I know it's getting late but I hope you can help me. I'm trying to find out the early history of the rail yards in downtown Brooklyn."

His face became a mass of wrinkles as he seemed to be trying to pull information out of the air.

"Well, you have two choices," he began in slow motion. "You can come back tomorrow or you can go across the street to Borough Hall and check with Topography. Gives you layouts, addresses, history." He bobbed his head as he spoke.

"Thanks. Thank you so much." She hurried out and darted across the street.

By the time she left Borough Hall, her heart and her mind were racing. She was so close to the ugly truth she could taste the sourness in her mouth. Her next stop was the Central Library on Grand Army Plaza. She needed all the history she could find.

Digging up facts was her specialty and she was damned good at it.

CHAPTER 24

Blake decided to come home early and surprise Savannah by having dinner ready and a nice bubble bath waiting, and something very sexy for her to lounge around in.

He'd stopped at the market on his way home and picked up fresh shrimp and scallops along with two pounds of mussels — one of Savannah's favorites. A bottle of cooking wine, angel-hair pasta, Italian bread and condiments rounded out his purchases.

Blake dropped the bags off in the kitchen then went directly to their bedroom to get out of his work clothes.

He took a quick shower, put on a pair of shorts and a T-shirt, then looked for the perfect outfit for his wife. Had he thought about it early enough he would have picked her up something new. But the truth was Savannah had more enticing little outfits than a department store. Shopping for lingerie was her personal fetish — and he loved it.

He chuckled to himself as he looked in the treasure chest. Some of the pieces still had price tags on them. He shook his head. It almost felt decadent going through her undies. Although they'd been married for years, he couldn't remember ever going in her drawers. Just as he thought he'd found the perfect set — a firebrand red, no more than sets of strings with frills — he noticed her Tender Loving Care carrying case buried under the layers of lingerie.

He started to close the drawer but curiosity coursed through his fingertips. He started to lift it out, just as the phone rang. He crossed the room and picked up the phone on the nightstand.

"Hello?"

"Blake, how are you?"

He gripped the phone. "I'm fine thank you. Why are you calling me at home?"

"I wanted to apologize about the other day in your office. What I did was truly out of line. Your secretary said you left early and —"

"Fine. Thanks for the apology. I've got to go."

"Blake, please . . . wait. I'm right in front of your house. I wanted to bring you a peace offering."

His chest tightened. In front of his house! "Look, it's not necessary."

"I know, but I want to. I'll sit right here all night if I have to." She laughed lightly. "I simply want to look you in the eye and say I'm sorry."

Blake rushed out of the bedroom and went up front then pulled back the curtain. There she was, waving to him from the window of her Town Car.

He slapped his palm against his forehead and let loose a string of curses. This was going to stop once and for all.

Dani pulled up across the street from Savannah and Blake's town house. She couldn't believe the nerve of this heifer. Worse, was Blake expecting her, thinking that Savannah was still at work?

When Tristan got out of the car and headed for the house, Dani's first reaction was to jump out and tackle the home wrecker to the ground. But she had on her good shoes and she'd just had her nails done — or it would have been on and poppin'.

Instead she called Nia.

"What?"

"Exactly. She's here, live and in living

239

color. Wait. Blake is coming to the door."
She whipped out her camera and started
shooting.

"Dani! Dani!" Nia yelled into the phone.
"What's going on?"

Dani put down the camera. "Looks like
Blake is pissed. I'm going over there."

"No! She doesn't need to see you — just
in case. You're on surveillance, remember?
See and not be seen."

"Damn!" Dani tapped her foot with impa-
tience. "Wait, looks like she's leaving and
she doesn't look like a happy camper."

"Blake has been redeemed," Nia murmured, relieved.

Dani checked the clock on the dash. It
was after six. Nick would be waiting. He
was always on time. "Look, I gotta go. I have
a date tonight and I'm already late."

"Another date? Same guy?"

"Maybe."

"What kind of answer is that?"

"The only one you're getting at the moment. Listen, let's all meet tomorrow after
work at The Shop."

"Let's do an early breakfast instead."

"Fine. Whatever. You call Savannah and
confirm. I overheard some stuff today at the
restaurant and maybe between the three of
us we can make some sense out of it."

"See you tomorrow. Enjoy your date."

"Thanks. I intend to."

Dani pulled off from the curb and used speed dial to call Nick. He picked up his cell on the second ring.

"I know. You're running late," he answered good naturedly.

Dani smiled. "Yeah, just a little. Where are you?"

"Camped out in front of your door, like a love-struck Romeo, while listening to Wendy Williams, they're playing that interview that she did with Whitney a couple of years ago." He chuckled. "What a mess."

Dang, she didn't even listen to Wendy. "I'll be there in about twenty minutes."

"No problem. I'll be here."

"See you soon." She disconnected the call and realized how much she wanted to see him.

When Savannah walked into her home about eight that evening, she'd already gotten the 4-1-1 from Nia and Dani about Tristan's visit to her house. If she'd had any qualms about crossing the line into Tristan's life before — all bets were off now.

She turned the key in the door and stepped in. Blake was on the couch looking as if he had news about Armageddon.

Savannah slowly put her purse down on the hall table and walked over to him.

"Blake, what is it?" She'd have to wait for him to tell her what she already knew. And he'd better tell her.

He glanced up at her. "We need to talk." He reached for her hand and eased her down beside him.

Please tell me the truth, she silently prayed.

"I was getting ready to surprise you with dinner and a hot bubble bath when Tristan Montgomery showed up — unannounced," he quickly added.

Savannah's eyes widened and her mouth dropped open. She leaped up from the chair and shot Blake a death gaze. "Don't even tell me she came into my house," she said, biting out every word for emphasis.

"No, she didn't, I made sure of that."

Savannah let the air out of her chest, smiling inside at her stellar performance.

"I'm contacting my attorney in the morning to see what my options are in terms of breaking this contract." He reached for her and pulled her down onto his lap. "I don't intend to spend the next two to three years that it's going to take to complete this job, under her thumb. I don't like being threatened. I'd rather lose the contract and deal with the loss than to ruin our life. Some things just aren't worth it. And I'm definitely not going to allow her to mess with my marriage. I don't give a damn how much money she has or what she can do to me." He paused and looked deep into her eyes. "Us, is the important thing, you and me."

Savannah's heart thundered with happiness. "We'll find a way to get through this." She stroked his cheek and rested her head against his chest.

"I know. I just have to figure out what I'm going to tell the crew."

"There will be other jobs, Blake."

"Let's hope so."

They sat wrapped around each other for several moments.

"Wow, the reason I came home early was to surprise you with dinner. I think I better get started."

"We'll do it together. Let me get changed." She kissed him lightly on the lips, stood then looked down at him. "Don't worry, okay? Everything is going to work out."

"From your lips . . ." he said, trying to put some cheer in his voice. He knew that if Tristan was as vindictive as she put on the next job for his company could be a long time coming.

Savannah walked off to the bedroom and stopped short. Her TLC case was on the bed. A cold sweat broke out on her forehead. Her head snapped toward the open door. Had he been in the case? Why was it out? Her thoughts ran at lightning speed. Even if he did open it, there was no way he could figure out what each of the items really was. Could he?

"Sorry, I was hunting for something sexy for you to wear during dinner."

She nearly jumped out of her skin. She slowly turned with a placid look on her face. "And you thought you'd find it in my cosmetics case?" she said, teasing, hoping that the tremors in her voice were only in her head.

Blake stepped in the room. "No." He looked embarrassed. "I found it when I was looking for an outfit for you." He frowned. "What's in there anyway, that you would keep it buried in the bottom of the drawer — top secrets?" He chuckled.

Her throat was suddenly as dry as sand. "Don't be silly. Top secrets." She laughed. "Yes, darling, the secrets to eternal beauty." She reached for the case and walked to her dresser and put it back. She shoved the drawer shut then turned to Blake with a smile plastered on her face. Her heart was beating so fast she could barely breathe.

Blake looked at her curiously. "You're

sweating. Want me to turn on the air?"

She swallowed. "Uh, no. I'm going to take a quick shower. Don't want to catch a chill."

"I'll get dinner started. I'd wanted to have a bubble bath ready for you but . . ."

"It's the thought that counts. I'll be out to help in a few minutes." She snatched up her robe from the foot of the bed and hustled off to the bathroom.

Once the door was shut she finally breathed. Blake was no fool. If he'd opened the case, which apparently he hadn't, it wouldn't have taken him too long to figure out that the cosmetics had no cosmetic value. Fortunately for the casual observer everything looked fine. There were a few authentic items in the case, but for the most part . . .

She'd have to be more careful in the future.

Savannah was the last to arrive at The Shop. Nia and Dani had secured a table in the back.

"Sorry I'm late — long night," she said, sliding into her seat.

"Long night as in good, or long night as in long?" Nia asked.

Savannah grinned thinking about the exquisite loving Blake had put on her the night

245

before. She was still tingling. "Long as in good — if you must know," she said with a wicked grin.

The trio laughed.

"Dang, seems like everyone had a hot evening except for me," Nia complained.

Savannah looked at Dani who had her eyes focused on her cup of tea. Savannah loudly cleared her throat. "And who was it?" she asked Dani.

"Just a guy."

"Yeah, just a guy that she's been on more than one date with," Nia added.

Dani looked at her and rolled her eyes. "Don't hate."

"Why not?" Nia said, biting into her bagel. "Anna has Blake and you have your mystery man. Who do I have?"

"Anyway," Dani said, dismissing Nia's blatant inquiry. "We're not here to discuss our love lives or lack thereof." She gave Nia a pointed look. Nia huffed. "We have real business to discuss."

"So, what did you two find out?" Savannah asked. She put her folder on the table.

"Well, it seems that Tristan and this Larry fellow — her attorney — are definitely in it together," Dani began. "There's been a lot of money changing hands since way before this deal for the development was signed."

She looked from one to the other. "She is well connected and has friends in very high places — the decision makers. And apparently, from what I could overhear, Larry has worked the contracts to protect Tristan. But the city council and the zoning commission are all involved up to their eyeballs."

"With all the gentrification going on in the area," Nia added, "and everyone gobbling up the prime real estate it was all about profit. None of them cared what happened to the people or the land as long as they get their cut." She opened a small notebook where she'd taken down the information that Desi had given her.

Savannah's lips pinched into a tight line when she read it. "Then it is true. Everything I found out yesterday and your information, Nia, and your take on the conversation, Dani, points to a major conspiracy not just to the people who have been displaced but to an entire heritage."

The all nodded in silent agreement.

Dani spoke up first. "So what are you going to do now? I can't imagine that anyone involved is going to let you go public with the information."

Savannah pushed out a long breath. "The groundbreaking is in three days. I'm going to compile all of the information that we have into one document and present it to Jean." She sighed. "She'll have to take it from there."

"Do you plan to tell Blake?" Nia asked.

"I may have to. I don't want him to be totally blindsided. This is bound to hit the news."

"Yeah, but how are you going to tell him you found out?" Dani asked.

"I'll think of something. It may be a moot point. He plans to talk to his attorney today to see how he can break the contract. If he does then I don't have to worry about it."

She checked her watch. "I have to get to the office." She looked from one face to the other. "Thanks, for everything. For being in my corner, for keeping this secret and for . . . just being my girls." She smiled warmly.

"Hey, if you can't share sex, lies and intrigue with your best friends, who can you share it with?" Dani joked.

"You're right about that." She stood and the room swayed. She gripped the edge of the table.

"You okay?" Nia asked, jumping to her feet.

Savannah shut her eyes for a minute and drew in a breath. "Yeah, fine. Lack of sleep and no food."

"Here, take the rest of my bagel," Dani offered. "Eat it in the car."

"Thanks." She took it from Dani and took a tentative bite. Her head and stomach slowly settled. "I'll talk to you guys later."

Dani and Nia watched her leave.

"Savannah lives on no sleep and lack of food when she's on a project for that crazy job of hers." She looked Dani in the eyes. "Are you thinking what I'm thinking?"

Dani slowly nodded her head and grinned. "Maybe we'll be aunties after all."

Blake sat opposite Frank Lloyd, the corporate attorney, in the conference room.

"This contract is airtight, Blake. I have to tell you that if you break it, she can sue you for everything you have and then some. You'll be ruined, financially and professionally. Is there no way you can see your way around dealing with Montgomery Enterprises?"

"No." He shook his head. "There has to be some clause, some loophole that I can slip through to get out of this without getting burned too badly."

"You would have to prove sexual harassment and that she threatened you. And at this point it's your word against hers. And I have to tell you, it would be a helluva case to try to prove in court."

Blake's shoulders slumped. Slowly he rose from his seat, chewing on his bottom lip as he thought of his options, which were zero to none.

"Have you talked to Steven about this?"

"He had a family crisis," he said absently.

"Is there anyone who can corroborate your allegations against Ms. Montgomery?"

Blake blew out a breath. "No."

Frank shut the folder. "If you want to proceed, I can put in the paperwork, but I'm warning you it will get ugly and you will be the one who will suffer. She'll find another developer and you will be finished."

Blake slung his hands into the pockets of his khakis. "I'll think of something and get back to you."

Frank gathered his things and stood. "You don't have much time."

"I know, I know."

"Call me. And whatever you decide, I'll take care of it."

"Thanks."

After Frank left, Blake placed a call to Steven. It was only fair that he told his business partner that they would soon be out of business unless a miracle happened.

CHAPTER 25

By the time Savannah arrived at her office she was feeling much better. She couldn't remember the last time she'd gotten light-headed. All the stress and pressure of the past couple of weeks were beginning to take their toll. That and having to keep secrets from Blake.

The moment she was settled at her desk, Richard showed up.

"So what did you find out?"

"Plenty," she said, reaching for her bag. She pulled out her notes on the house in Westchester. "I'll get them all typed up and have it to you in about an hour."

"How does it look for our clients?"

"According to everything that I've found out, our clients will be very happy landowners."

Richard grinned. "Now, that's the kind of news I like to hear. I knew I could depend on you. Thanks, as always."

"My pleasure."

He turned to leave. "Bring the info in when you're done so we can go over it together."

"Sure," she called out.

Her phone rang.

"Billings and Tate, Savannah speaking."

"Hey, sweetheart, it's Mom."

"Hi, Mom."

"How is everything going?"

"Turned out to be a little bit more than I bargained for, but I'm just about to wrap everything up."

"How are things with you and Blake?"

"Great."

"You're not just saying that to shut me up, are you?"

"Shut *you* up! Never." She laughed. "But seriously, things are fine between me and Blake."

"Good." She paused. "I thought we could meet for lunch. I was going to do some shopping and I'll be in your neck of the woods."

"I'd like that. How about one?"

"Perfect. Can I meet you in the lobby of your building?"

"Sure. I'll see you at one."

"Goodbye, sweetheart. I'll see you soon."

" 'Bye, Mom."

Savannah slowly hung up the phone. Spending an hour with her mom might be just the medicine she needed. Her mom, always pragmatic, would have the best advice on how she should proceed. After all Claudia was a card-carrying member of the Cartel. Savannah grinned and shook her head. Who would have ever thought it?

In the meantime, she needed to compile her information for Richard. But before she did she needed to listen to the recordings from Tristan's home and office. There wasn't a moment to check the night before and just maybe there was something she could use.

She pulled out her PDA, put on her headset and scrolled to her audio program. While it went through the registry process, she turned on her computer and began putting together the draft of information for Richard. Finally the program was fully loaded and the audio began.

The first set of conversations was in Tristan's home. Nothing of major interest. Then, just when she was getting bored, Tristan made a call to her girlfriend.

". . . I went to his office and got practically naked in front of him and he wouldn't bite," Tristan was saying.

"Girl, are you out of your mind? Suppose

a secretary or somebody had come in?"

"I didn't care. I just wanted him."

"Maybe you need to just give up and move on. The man is apparently in love with his wife and the only reason why you want him is because he belongs to someone else."

"That's not true! Well, maybe a little. But from the first time I saw his profile in *Black Enterprise* magazine I set my sights on him. I could have chosen dozens of other architectural developers, but I chose him."

"Now you need to un-choose him. It's not working. At least not the way you want it to."

"You know I don't give up. I have him backed into a corner."

"What are you talking about now?"

"I told him plain and simple that if he doesn't satisfy my carnal needs, I'd ruin him." She laughed. "And you know I will."

Bingo!

Her friend chuckled. "Tristan you are a mess. You need your head examined."

"No, what I need is a taste of what Mrs. Fields gets every night."

"What if you go through all of this and he's lousy in bed? Looks are deceiving, you know."

Tristan laughed. "Trust me, I know a good man when I see one. It's like picking out shoes. You know the ones you want and even if they don't fit perfectly, they still look good with that outfit. You simply work them into shape."

"Yeah, well, you tell me how it fits — if you ever find out."

"Oh, I will. Blake is not going to let his entire business go down the toilet over something as simple as a long roll in the sack."

"If you say so. I gotta go, hubby just came home and we have dinner reservations. I'll talk to you soon."

" 'Bye."

The call disconnected. Savannah's emotions vacillated between outright fury and vindication. She finally had what she needed to nail that wench and get Blake off the hook. The trick now was how she was going to use the information without Blake finding out what she'd been up to.

Maybe her mom would have some answers. She saved the audio recording on a portable flash drive. It certainly wouldn't do to lose this tasty bit of information. She popped the flash drive into its case and put it in her purse.

One o'clock couldn't get here fast enough.

They were seated in an outdoor café across

the street from Lincoln Center. The day was gorgeous, with a warm breeze and clear blue skies, and the view of the center with its magnificent fountain could almost make Savannah forget all the things that weighed so heavily on her mind.

Savannah was ravenous. Her stomach growled and grumbled as she studied the menu. Everything looked good and she felt as if she could eat it all.

"I feel as if I haven't seen you in forever," Claudia said, setting her dark shades on the table.

As always Claudia was totally en vogue. Her two-piece designer suit in pale peach was stunning on her. And of course, her nails and hair were done to perfection. Savannah felt almost dowdy in her tailored gray business suit.

"I know it has been a while since we've had a chance to talk."

Claudia glanced up at the waitress who approached their table. "I'll have a bottle of spring water, a glass with no ice and a piece of lemon. And for my meal I'll have the seared salmon salad." She handed her menu to the waitress.

Savannah wanted the steak and potatoes but thought about the pounds. "Make that two." She handed over her menu, as well.

Claudia tilted her head to the side and looked at her daughter. "Your eyes are sparkling and your skin looks beautiful."

"Really? I hadn't noticed."

Claudia didn't comment further but steered the conversation to the matters at hand. "So, tell me how the case is coming along."

"There's so much to tell, I hardly know where to begin."

"Just give me the highlights and I'll fill in the blanks."

Savannah pushed out a long breath and leaned forward, lowering her voice. "Well . . ."

By the time Savannah had finished telling her mother everything that had gone on since she took the case, they'd completed their meal and the waitress was presenting the check.

Claudia's light brown eyes were cinched into tight slits. "I can't believe the nerve of that woman. And now Blake has to pay the cost." She roughly shook her head. "At least with all the details you have about the construction site, Jean can take care of that. Not a brick will be laid without a full and complete investigation. It's just sick what people are capable of." She rubbed her mouth with the napkin then zeroed in on

Savannah. "Your issue is this woman and your husband. If he pulls out before Jean can launch a halt, Tristan will do what she's threatened. That much I'm sure of. It's your marriage that I'm concerned about."

"I have the tape out of her own mouth saying how she tried to seduce him and blackmail him into complying. I just don't know how I can use the information without Blake finding out."

Claudia mulled it over. "Listen, forget about the job, and forget about politics. Think about this as one woman up against another. If the assignment wasn't involved and some woman was trying to take your husband, what would you do?"

"I would be in her face with what I knew."

Claudia slapped her palm on the table. "Exactly. You're going to take that recording and march yourself up to her office and let her hear what you have on her."

"She's going to want to know how I found out."

"Do you really care what she wants to know? The facts are the facts. Lay them on the table and dare her to bluff her way out of it. You have the trump card."

A surge of excitement rushed through Savannah. Of course, this went beyond some shady land dealings. This was her marriage. This was her man. And if Tristan wanted to fight dirty, so could she.

She focused on her mother's steady gaze, a slow grin moved across her mouth. "I'll let you know what happened." She started to get up from the table. "Thanks, Mom." She leaned down and kissed her soft cheek, then put forty dollars on the table. "Advice on you, lunch on me. Talk to you soon." She turned to leave.

"Oh, and Savannah . . ."

She stopped. "Yes?"

"Make an appointment with your doctor."

Savannah frowned. "Why?"

"Just do it."

Savannah shrugged it off and hurried back to her office. She'd have to come up with some excuse to see Tristan again, but she'd think of something. And she'd have to make it quick, she didn't want Blake to lose his company before she could play her cards. She'd just have to come up with some excuse when she got back to the office as to why she had to leave early — again.

But first things first. She needed to make sure that Blake hadn't done anything crazy. She called him from her cell phone on her way back to her office.

"Hi, Savannah, Blake is out of the office for the rest of the day," his secretary said.

"You should probably be able to reach him on his cell."

"Did he say where he was going?"

"No, only that he had some business to take care of out of the office and he wouldn't be back."

"Okay, thanks. If he should call before I reach him, please tell him to call me. It's important."

"Sure thing."

"Thanks." She quickly disconnected and put in Blake's cell-phone number. It rang and rang then went to voice mail. She left a quick message to call her and hung up. Where in the world was he and why wasn't he answering his phone?

CHAPTER 26

Blake thought about hashing it all out with Steven on the phone but this was something they needed to discuss face-to-face. They'd built the business together and he had every right to know exactly what was going on and what they were on the precipice of losing.

Maybe by some miracle, Steve could see some way out of it that he couldn't.

Traffic leading into and through the Holland Tunnel was hellacious. He'd been sitting inside the tunnel for fifteen minutes. It was apparent that there had to be an accident or something up ahead. He put the car in Neutral and waited, growing increasingly impatient, although there was nothing he could do about it. To make matters worse he couldn't even listen to the radio. All he got was static. He should have listened to Savannah when she'd told him long ago to pack some CDs in the car. At this rate it would be nightfall by the time he arrived in New Jersey.

He should have called her before he left so that she wouldn't worry and to update her on his plans. He picked up his cell phone and saw the icon for no signal. He tossed it onto the passenger seat. Figures.

Finally the traffic began to creep forward. Another twenty minutes and he finally hit daylight. He surged ahead, not wanting to waste any more time. He'd call Savannah once he finally reached Steve's sister's house.

Savannah returned to her office still mulling over what story she needed to come up with to leave early and get to Tristan's office before the end of the day. She'd been listening in on Tristan's office conversations on her walk back to her office and knew that Tristan would be there at least until six.

Just as she stepped off the elevator she ran smack into Richard.

"Oh, Savannah. Glad I ran into you," he joked. "I'm heading out to Westchester to meet with the client and bring them up to date on what you found out."

"Great. Uh . . ."

"And for doing such a great job, why don't you take the rest of the afternoon off?

Things are pretty quiet and I don't need you for anything right now."

"Wow, thanks."

"Sure." He stepped onto the elevator. "See you in the morning."

The elevator doors swooshed shut.

Savannah grinned. That couldn't have worked out better if she'd planned it herself. She hurried to her desk, shut down her computer and collected her things.

Moments later she was pulling out of the employee parking lot and heading to Tristan's office. On the way over, she tried Blake on his cell one more time. Finally he picked up.

"Hey, did you get my message?"

"No, I was stuck in the tunnel. What's up?"

"The tunnel?"

"Yeah, I'm on my way to see Steven. I met with Frank this morning and he doesn't see how I can get out of this contract without losing my shirt. I want to talk to Steven about it."

"You haven't said anything to Tristan yet, have you?" Her heart pounded.

"No. I didn't think it would be fair to not talk to Steven first."

She released a sigh. "Well, you two discuss it. I'm sure something will work out."

"I hope so, babe, just not sure what. Anyway, I'll see you at home later tonight."

"Drive safe."

"Thanks. Love you."

"Love you, too." Savannah disconnected the call. Well, at least she had some time to put her own plan into action. Trump Tower loomed ahead.

She turned her car over to the valet and hurried inside. She had the tape recording of Tristan's late-night conversation in her purse. Two could play at this dirty game.

"I need to see Ms. Montgomery," she said to the receptionist, which was a different woman since the last time she was there.

"Do you have an appointment?"

"No. But it's important. Can you please tell her that Mrs. Fields is here and it's about the rail-yard project?"

"I'm really sorry, but she's in meetings all afternoon. If you want to leave a message I'll be sure to get it to her as soon as she's done."

Savannah braced her palms on the desk and leaned forward. "Tell her I want to see her now. If not, the information I have will be on the news instead of in her hands. Got it?"

The woman flicked backward. Without taking her eyes off Savannah, she pressed a button on the phone and talked through her headset.

"Sorry to disturb you, Ms. Montgomery, but there is a Mrs. Fields here to see you and she says it's urgent."

"I know, ma'am, I told her. She said —" she lowered her voice "— either she gives the information to you or the press."

"Yes, ma'am." She pursed her lips before speaking. "She said you can wait here. She'll be out shortly."

"Thank you."

Savannah turned on her heel and took a seat on the white leather sofa, tapping her foot while she waited.

About ten minutes later, Tristan strutted down the corridor to Savannah. She was stunned once again by Tristan's beauty, but she wasn't going to get distracted by looks or let her own insecurities rear their ugly heads. This was war.

She stood.

"What is this about?" Tristan demanded, pinning Savannah with a hard gaze.

"I think it best if we talk in private. Unless you want your staff to overhear what I have to say."

Tristan's jaw clenched. She whirled away and headed toward her office. Savannah followed.

"You have two minutes and then I'm calling security." She folded her arms and stared at Savannah.

Savannah went into her purse and took out the tape recorder. She placed it on the table.

"What the hell is this?"

"Listen, and you'll find out."

Savannah pressed Play.

Within moments, Tristan's voice, clear as a bell, could be heard detailing her escapade to her friend.

Tristan's cool features went frigid. Her eyes widened. She glared at Savannah.

"What the hell? Where did you get that?"

"It really doesn't matter where I got it. The point is I have it. And if you even think about messing with my husband again, or his business, this little baby will be all over the six-o'clock news. I'm sure it won't sit well with your board members or all of your big-shot friends."

Tristan's chest heaved in and out. "What do you want?" she finally said.

"I want you to stay the hell away from my husband. Period. And if you think for a New York minute that I'm bluffing, try me."

Tristan slowly lowered herself into her chair. Finally she looked at Savannah. "Fine. Now, give me the tape."

Savannah tossed her head back and laughed. "I may not travel in high society, but I'm not a fool. This is my insurance. You do your part and I'll do mine. But if I even think in my sleep that you have him on your mind, I will make this tape public. Do we understand each other?"

Tristan's nostrils flared. "Yes. Now, please leave."

"With pleasure." She snatched up the recorder and walked out.

As she walked down the corridor to the elevator she had the heart-pounding feeling that at any second security was going to snatch her up and make her disappear. She didn't breathe easy until she'd gotten outside, behind the wheel of her car and was halfway home.

The first thing she did when she arrived was to make copies of every piece of evidence that she had. There were barely two days left before the groundbreaking. She needed to have all her ducks in a row when she presented her information to Jean.

She called her mother.

"How did it go?"

"It couldn't have gone better."

"Great," Claudia cheered. "I'm proud of you. At least you have her in a holding pattern until Jean can work things on her end."

267

"That's the reason why I called. I was hoping you could come by for an hour or so before Blake gets here and help me put all of this information together. You've done this before and I could use your help. I don't want anything to be overlooked or not have all that I need to present a strong case."

"I can be there in about twenty minutes."

"Great. Blake is in New Jersey. I don't expect him back until later on tonight."

"See you in a few."

With that bit of business out of the way, Savannah finally sighed in a moment of relief. It was all coming together. Blake would be able to keep his business, the building would cease and a full investigation launched and, best of all, her marriage was as solid as a rock.

Savannah darted into the kitchen and hunted around in the fridge for some quick leftovers. She was starving. She found a pot of black beans and rice and some fried chicken. She put it all into a bowl and popped it in the microwave. The three-minute warm-up time seemed to take an eternity. Her head started to spin. She went to the table and sat down.

Maybe she did need to see a doctor. She'd been feeling weird all day. Once all of this was over she was sure she'd feel better. If

268

not she would take her mother's advice and make an appointment.

The bell chimed on the microwave and in minutes, she'd devoured the plate of food, just as the doorbell rang.

"Your mouth is greasy," Claudia said as she came through the door.

"Oh, I just finished eating some fried chicken." She wiped the corners of her mouth with her fingers.

Claudia breezed inside. "Where do you have everything?"

"In the bedroom."

"Bring it all out here. That way we can hear Blake when he comes in."

"Good idea." She went to the bedroom and retrieved all of the information and the tapes she'd made.

For the next hour they organized all of the data.

"They are going to want to see a list of everyone who may be involved, along with dates and times that this information was gathered. That's just to insure that nothing has been doctored."

Savannah nodded, and culled through her paperwork and the data on her PDA and BlackBerry. She plugged the PDA into her laptop and connected that to the printer and it spit out the list and timetable.

The last piece of damning evidence was what she'd received from the library and the Topography office.

"It totally blows my mind that no one has said anything about this," Savannah said.

"If the right people were paid enough money why would they talk?"

"I guess you're right. Funny, Jean wanted me to investigate Tristan for what she thought was substandard contracting and under the table payments. But this . . ." She shook her head.

"It's going to make the news. And of course, you can never tell anyone of your involvement."

"I know."

Claudia brushed her daughter's hair with her hand. "You did good, Savannah. Real good."

Savannah smiled like a proud child. "Thanks. So many things got in the middle of this. I really didn't think I would pull it off."

"But you did. And you are going to make history."

"Yeah, even if I can't take the credit for it."

"But you'll know it in your heart and generations will be thanking you for it. Now, you need to transfer all of the data into one location and burn it onto a CD. Make two copies. One for Jean and one for safekeeping."

"Right. I'll do that now."

"Then you need to call Jean and let her know what you have. I'm sure she'll want to see you right away."

They'd taken care of all the details and Savannah had placed a high-priority call to Jean. She and her mother were just settling down for a glass of wine when Blake came through the door.

Savannah got up to greet him. She wrapped her arms around his waist and kissed him long and slow on his lips.

"Hmm, and what did I do to deserve that?" His eyes sparkled. He pulled her close.

"Love me," she whispered.

"That's the easy part." He dipped his head to take her mouth again when Claudia loudly cleared her throat.

Blake's head popped up. "Claudia. I didn't know you were here."

"Apparently," she said with a chuckle. "I was just leaving. Came to see about my daughter." She picked up her purse from the coffee table and walked toward the door.

Blake pecked her on the cheek. "Sure you

don't want to stay?"

She looked wickedly from one to the other. "And mess up the good time you two are planning to have. I don't think so, sweetheart."

Heat rushed to Savannah's face. She never would get over how blunt her mother could be when it came to sex.

"I'll talk to you soon, Savannah."

" 'Night, Mom. Thanks for stopping by."

Claudia wagged a finger at her son-in-law. "And you, young man, need to check the premises before you go jumping on your wife." She laughed and walked out.

"Whew, your mom . . ." He let the comment hang in the air.

Savannah held up her hand. "I know, don't say it." She took his hand and led him inside.

They settled down on the couch.

"So what happened with Steven?"

Blake draped his arm across the back of the couch and played in her hair. "He agrees with me. We'll take the hit and hope to beat it in court."

She swallowed. "Do you trust me?"

His brow knitted. "Of course. Why?"

She tugged on her bottom lip with her teeth. "If I ask you not to say anything to Tristan for at least two days and not ask me

272

any questions, would you do it?"

"Savannah, what's going on? The ground-breaking is day after tomorrow. I need to disconnect myself and my company from the project before then. Maybe if you tell me why —"

"Please just trust me. Okay, not two days. Wait until tomorrow evening. Please."

"It would really help your case 'counselor' if you told me why."

She put a finger to his lips. "No questions."

He heaved a sigh. "Okay. No questions and I'll wait until tomorrow, end of business. No later. I'll have to prepare a press release to send to the media by then."

"Fair enough."

"I'd feel a lot better if I knew why I was holding off on the announcement."

"Trust me, everything will be fine. Hungry?"

He rubbed his stomach. "I could use some food."

Savannah chuckled. "I'll see what I can whip together. I'm pretty hungry myself," she said, and wondered why. She'd eaten less than two hours earlier.

While Savannah was in the kitchen she heard her cell phone. "Honey, could you answer that for me?" she yelled out.

A moment later he came into the kitchen mouthing, "Jean." He handed her the phone.

"Thanks."

Blake stood there.

"It's the head of TLC, probably wants to talk to me about my next order," she said, pressing the phone to her chest.

He opened the fridge and took out an apple then went to the sink and washed it off. "Don't mind me, I'm going. I'll let you ladies talk about your secret beauty products." He chuckled, took a bite from the apple and returned to the living room.

Shortly Savannah heard the television. He was watching CNN.

"Hello, Jean, sorry for the wait."

"I got your message. I need you to bring all of the documents to me right away."

"Now?"

"Yes. We don't have any time to waste."

"But I can't leave. My husband's home. What am I going to tell him? I have the information on a CD. I can e-mail it to you."

"No. The file is too large. I'll send a messenger. It will be someone that you know. Give the package to them."

"Okay."

"And, Savannah . . ."

"Yes?"

"If this all pans out . . . well, we'll see. Good night. I'll be in touch."

Savannah hung up and she could almost hear the James Bond theme song playing in the background.

She stepped out into the living room. Blake was engrossed in the news and didn't notice her. She went straight into the bedroom, took the envelope out of her carryall and brought it with her back to the kitchen. In the event that she needed some kind of excuse to go out and meet the driver, she'd just say she was taking out the garbage.

In the meantime, she still needed to fix something for dinner. She stood staring inside the refrigerator totally unable to decide. So many things were running through her head at once she couldn't think clearly.

Frustrated she trooped back into the living room and plopped down next to Blake.

"How about if we order in? I can't figure out what to fix."

"Fine with me. What are you in the mood for?"

"Mexican?"

"Cool. Get me whatever you're having," he said, surfing over to a tennis game.

She pushed up from the couch and went

to get the menu from the kitchen drawer just as the doorbell rang.

Savannah's heart pounded in her chest. A wave of heat suddenly rushed through her and the room swayed. She grabbed on to the counter.

"I'll get it!" Blake called out. "Are you expecting anyone?"

She drew in deep breaths to clear her head. "Huh?"

"Never mind. I got it."

Savannah shook her head and moved toward the door. It was probably whomever Jean sent. Gosh, what was wrong with her? She stepped out into the foyer, just as Blake was closing the door.

"Mom?"

"Hi. Silly me. I left my envelope with my TLC orders." She gave Savannah a pointed look.

"Oh . . . yes, you sure did. I noticed it in the kitchen. I'll get it for you."

Claudia followed Savannah.

"Jean sent *you?*" Savannah said under her breath.

"Yep. Surprised?"

"Nothing surprises me anymore." She took the envelope from the top of the fridge. "That's everything."

"You have your copies?"

"Yes."

"Good. I'm sure you'll be hearing from Jean the minute she goes through everything." She headed for the door. "Good night again, Blake."

" 'Night," he called out from his spot on the couch.

"Talk to you tomorrow," Claudia said. "Be prepared for the fireworks, and I do mean in the bedroom. I saw that look in Blake's eyes." She winked and walked out.

Savannah pinched her lips together and shut the door behind her mother. There was just no telling what Claudia might say.

"Did Mom get everything?"

"Mmm, hmm." She sat down next to Blake.

"So what did you order for dinner?"

"I didn't. I'll do it now." She started to get up.

Blake caught her wrist. "Are you okay? You look flushed or something."

"I'm okay. Just tired, I guess, and it's catching up with me."

"Let's eat. Then I'll give you an all over body massage. How's that sound?"

Savannah cuddled next to him. "Sounds wonderful." She yawned.

"You order, I'll run you a hot bath. Okay."

She nodded and yawned again. Blake

pushed up from the couch and handed her the phone. "You want me to put anything special in the water?"

She looked up at him with a crooked smile. "Yeah, you."

"Don't have to ask me twice."

Savannah rested her head against the back of the couch and shut her eyes. By this time tomorrow this would all be over and she could stop lying to her husband and sneaking around. At least for now. Her stomach growled. She dialed the restaurant and placed the order. Maybe she was going to have to stop taking those vitamins.

She went into the bedroom and was greeted by the scent of mango coming from the master bath. She poked her head in the open doorway.

Blake was sitting on the edge of the tub testing the water. He looked up. "Hey, gorgeous. Bath is almost ready."

She came inside and drew in a long deep breath inhaling the sweet steam then looked down at him. She slowly unbuttoned her blouse and tossed it to the floor. Her skirt followed.

"Still planning to join me?" she said, unsnapping her bra. She dropped it on the growing pile.

Blake's eyes darkened. He stood. "You want to do the honors?"

The corner of Savannah's mouth curved upward. "With pleasure . . ."

Chapter 27

The following morning as Savannah and Blake were preparing for work, the news played in the background.

Savannah was sitting on the side of the bed when the *Today Show* was interrupted with a special bulletin.

The scene flashed to downtown Brooklyn.

"Blake. Isn't that the construction site?"

He stopped buttoning his shirt and focused on the television.

"We're here at the construction site that was scheduled for the groundbreaking tomorrow. But according to reports, that's not going to happen. The city was given official notice this morning to cease any work in this area. It seems that information received by the Department of Design and Construction late last night indicates that this is holy ground — an ancient African burial site."

Savannah's pulse was racing as she listened.

Blake's head snapped in Savannah's direction. She hoped she looked shocked.

"Sources close to the investigation have informed us that Tristan Montgomery of Montgomery Enterprises, the entity that financed and pushed through the development, was well aware of what she was building on and that certain city officials knew, as well. We have been unable to reach Ms. Montgomery for comment."

"Whoa." Blake dropped down beside Savannah on the bed.

"This location was touted to be the one to revitalize downtown Brooklyn. It took several years to get approval for building and to move out hundreds of families in the surrounding area. This is a major blow to Montgomery Enterprises, and with allegations of cover-ups and coercion, this is something that is not likely to go away soon. This is Geri Castle in downtown Brooklyn. Back to you, Matt."

"African burial grounds," Blake said in awe. Slowly he shook his head. "How could she have known and still want to build?"

"Money was obviously more important than the preservation of our history," Savannah said with distaste.

"I wonder how they finally found out?"

Savannah shrugged. "Who knows? I'm just glad that they did. And I'm glad that you didn't have to cancel the contract. Now you're off the hook and you can move on." She took his hand. "See, I told you things would work themselves out."

He looked at her curiously. "You were pretty sure, weren't you?"

She averted her gaze. "I have faith — in you." She kissed him lightly on the lips. "I wonder what they are going to do with the area now."

"We won't know, I'm sure, until they do a thorough investigation. But to think that our ancestors are buried there."

"The same thing happened in Manhattan a few years back, remember?"

He nodded. "True. It's just when you think of slavery, you think of the South. We tend to forget that slavery had a history right here in New York."

"Exactly." She stood and put her arms around his waist. "I love you. So very much."

"What brought that on?"

"Just everything. It's been a crazy few weeks and we came through it. Together."

"I'm really sorry that I put you through all that madness with Tristan."

"It wasn't your fault."

"I never want you to doubt me."

"I don't."

His eyes danced over her face. "There's something about you that's different. I don't know what it is."

"Is it good or bad?"

"Good. You're glowing."

"I'm happy."

"Well, it shows." He kissed the tip of her nose. "I better get out of here. I know it's going to be crazy at the office and I can imagine the phone calls from the press."

"Okay, get going. Call me later if you get a chance."

"I will."

The minute Blake left for work, Savannah called the girls. Then she made an appointment with her doctor. She didn't want to say anything until she was sure, but the little stick turned blue.

"We did it," Dani said, as the trio sat around the table at The Shop.

"We sure did. And I hope that conniving woman gets what she deserves," Nia added.

"I couldn't have done it without the both of you. And I really appreciate you guys."

They raised their teacups and toasted.

"So what happens now?" Dani asked.

Savannah shrugged. "I guess they'll investigate. Tristan and some folks on the city council and the zoning board will probably be brought up on charges. This is a major scandal."

"How is Blake handling it all?" Nia asked.

"He was stunned to say the least. But I know he's glad it's over and he's in the clear."

"So what's our next assignment?" Dani asked with a grin.

"You two weren't even supposed to be involved. If they ever found out, I'd probably get kicked out of the Cartel."

"So we can be your double secret agents," Nia joked.

"Yeah, right. I think I'm going to take a break for a minute and recoup from this little adventure." She looked from one face to the other. "It was kind of exciting, though."

They giggled.

"Yeah, I can really get into this spy stuff," Nia said. "Covert ops."

They all cracked up laughing.

"Hey, I gotta run. Let's get together this weekend," Savannah said.

"Sure. And, there's someone I want you both to meet," Dani said.

Nia and Savannah looked at each other.

"So, uh, why don't we do brunch on Sunday at my place?"

"Sure," they said in unison.

"And bring Blake if you want."

"What about me?" Nia whined.

"You'll be the fifth wheel as usual," Dani teased.

Nia socked her in the arm. "Not funny."

"Well, you two duke it out. I gotta go. I'll bring Mom. She'll round out the playing field. See ya."

As Savannah headed off to work she passed a newsstand. The headlines were glaring and so very satisfying.

Montgomery Enterprises On The Brink Of Collapse. The New Enron. Federal Investigation.

Savannah smiled. She'd done good.

CHAPTER 28

"I'm only doing this because I love you," Blake said as they headed for the door. "You know Sunday is sports day. I'm supposed to be on the couch." He snatched her around the waist. "And you're supposed to be there with me." He kissed her, gently at first then let his tongue dance along the curve of her lips until he felt her shudder just a bit in his arms. Tentatively he eased back. "See, we could stay here and . . ."

"No, you promised. Besides I want everyone together."

"Okay fine. Just for you."

"Is Steve going to meet us there?"

"Yeah, I gave him the address. I still can't believe he's never met Nia."

"I think they'd be perfect for each other. Steve needs to settle down and Nia needs a good man."

"If you say so."

"I do. Now, come on and let's go. Everyone else is probably there already."

"Does Dani have ESPN?" he asked, trailing behind her.

Savannah glanced over her shoulder and rolled her eyes.

Just as Savannah predicted, they were the last ones to arrive. And she couldn't have been more surprised if Martin Luther King had been sitting in her living room.

She glided in on Blake's arm.

Dani hurried over. "Close your mouth," she whispered. "Let me introduce you." She took Savannah by the hand and led her over to meet Nick who was in deep conversation with Claudia.

"Nick, I want you to meet my other best friend, Savannah Fields, and her husband, Blake."

Nick stood up and shook Savannah's hand and then Blake's. "Dani talks about you all the time. Glad to finally meet you both."

"Thanks. So how long have you known Dani?" Savannah asked.

Blake nudged her.

Nick looked to Dani. "How long has it been, babe? Seems like only yesterday," he teased.

"Don't mind him," Dani cut in. She took Savannah by the hand. "Come with me in the kitchen, will ya?"

"So, what do you think?" Dani asked the instant they were alone.

"I think he's gorgeous, for starters. But it's not about what I think. What do you think?"

Dani looked vulnerable for the first time that Savannah could remember. "I think I'm in love with him." She looked at her friend. "And it's scary."

"Oh, Danielle." She wrapped her in a hug. "Love is scary. It's supposed to be. That's what makes it so exciting."

"Hey, can I get a hug?" Nia came into the kitchen.

Dani sniffed back tears.

"We were talking about Dani's new man," Savannah offered. "Our girl is in love."

"Ain't he fine?" Nia said. "No wonder she's been keeping him under wraps."

"Is that the only reason?" Savannah asked gently.

"I . . . I wasn't sure what you guys would think. I wasn't even sure myself."

"None of that matters, girl. As long as he treats you right and treats us right, he can hang," Nia teased.

Dani chuckled. "Thanks, ya'll. That means a lot."

"And thanks for bringing Steve," Nia said.

"He's another cutie pie and really nice."

"Steve's a great guy. He just needs a great woman," Savannah said.

"How ya'll gonna leave me in there with those men?" Claudia said, busting in.

" 'Cause we know you could handle them, Mom."

"Well, I'm starving. When are we going to eat?"

"Right now. It's buffet so everyone can help themselves."

The group filed into the kitchen and heaped their plates with fried salmon patties, chicken fingers, yellow rice, salad and fresh fruit. Then they settled in the living room where the men had commandeered the television.

The doorbell rang.

"Oh, I'll get it," Claudia announced. She went to the door and all eyes followed her.

She returned with a dead ringer for a young and virile Billie Dee Williams.

"Everyone, I'd like you to meet my friend Bernard Hassel. Bernard, this is everyone."

Savannah stared at her mother dumbfounded.

"I thought we were more than friends," Bernard said in that same Billie Dee voice. Claudia giggled like a schoolgirl.

"Bernie, behave yourself. We don't want

to give these young folks the wrong idea." She took him by the hand and led him to an available seat.

One by one introductions were made while Claudia went to fix Bernard a plate.

Laughter and chatter filled the air, as potent as the smell of all that good food. The atmosphere was filled with friendship, love and happiness.

"I have an announcement to make," Savannah shouted over the din. "Well, *we* have an announcement to make." She grabbed Blake's hand. "We're going to have a baby."

Dani and Nia jumped and squealed. "I knew it!" they said in unison.

"A mother knows," Claudia chimed in, beaming like a proud grandma. "I told you."

"Congratulations, man," Steven said, slapping Blake on the back. "You did it." He laughed.

"Very funny." Blake chuckled.

Nick came over and shook Blake's hand and kissed Savannah's cheek. "Congratulations."

"If it's a girl I hope she's as beautiful as your mother," Bernard offered, hugging Claudia.

Claudia looked up at him with adorning eyes.

"This calls for a toast," Dani announced.

Everyone grabbed a glass.

"To Anna and Blake."

"To love and happiness."

"Friendship."

"New beginnings."

"To shopping for baby clothes!"

"Cheers!"

"I had a great time today," Blake admitted to Savannah as they lay in bed together.

"So did I." She rested her head on his shoulder. "We're having a baby," she whispered in awe.

"I know." He stroked her arm. "I told you it would happen. You just have to have faith."

She tilted her face up to him. "Yeah, how about that."

Tenderly he kissed her, and held her like spun glass, suddenly afraid of hurting her.

"I won't break," she whispered.

"Are you sure . . . it's all right?"

"The doctor said I'm fine. I'm only six weeks. Ask me again in about seven months."

"In that case . . ." He eased the straps from her gown off her shoulders and kissed her right in the valley of her neck then let his tongue trail across her bare shoulder.

Savannah moaned softly, letting her fingers play along the muscles in his back.

His head drifted down to the swell of her breasts until his tongue flicked across the peak of her nipple.

Instinctively her body arched toward him. He took the nipple into his mouth and spent the next hour loving every inch of her body.

Savannah didn't think it was possible to feel this exquisite, to have so many incredible sensations rushing through her at once. Every inch of her was electrified. And when Blake finally entered her body she knew heaven.

Epilogue

"Thank you for coming in, Savannah," Jean said from behind her ornate desk.

"Sure." She took a seat.

"You did an incredible job on your first assignment and I wanted to congratulate you personally."

"Thank you. That means a great deal."

"I know it must have been difficult for you to have to investigate your own husband."

"You knew all along, didn't you?"

"Of course. It's why I chose you. I had to see if you had what it took."

"You could have been wrong."

Jean gave her a pointed look. "I'm never wrong." She flipped open a folder and briefly looked it over. "I have another assignment for you." She closed the folder and pushed it toward Savannah. "With the baby on the way, you may want to engage the services of . . . your friends."

Savannah smiled.

ABOUT THE AUTHOR

Donna Hill began writing novels in 1990. Since that time she's had more than forty full-length novels and novellas published. Two of her novels and one novella were adapted for television. She has won numerous awards for her body of work. She is also the editor of five novels, two of which were nominated for awards. She easily moves from romance to erotica, horror, comedy and women's fiction. She was the first recipient of a Trailblazer award, and currently teaches writing at the Frederick Douglass Creative Arts Center. Donna lives in Brooklyn with her family. Visit her Web site at www.donnahill.com.

The employees of Thorndike Press hope you have enjoyed this Large Print book. All our Thorndike, Wheeler, and Kennebec Large Print titles are designed for easy reading, and all our books are made to last. Other Thorndike Press Large Print books are available at your library, through selected bookstores, or directly from us.

For information about titles, please call:
(800) 223-1244

or visit our Web site at:
http://gale.cengage.com/thorndike

To share your comments, please write:
Publisher
Thorndike Press
295 Kennedy Memorial Drive
Waterville, ME 04901